NO TEARS

Tales from the Square Mile

David Charters

Elliott & Thompson
London & Bath

To the best of them,
for the friendship and the good times.
And to the worst of them,
for the inspiration.

CONTENTS

Acknowledgements

I would like to thank a number of people who have helped me in putting this collection together.

My friend and colleague, John Mclaren, first encouraged me to put pen to paper, and helped and guided me throughout the process. Nick Webb helped convince me I should persevere, and introduced me to David Elliott and Brad Thompson, who shaped the final version. Jeremy Bailey, Roger Lewis, Steve McCauley and Adam Shutkever gave freely of their time to comment and to encourage me, and most of all my wife, Luisa, supported me throughout the process.

INTRODUCTION

The City of London can be a wonderful place. I spent twelve mostly happy years there. When I arrived as a refugee from the Foreign Office smarter men than me took a bet that I would succeed and hired me. I worked first at what was then SG Warburg Securities, then moved to Morgan Grenfell, which duly evolved into Deutsche Morgan Grenfell and finally took on the corporate identity of Deutsche Bank.

The City was good to me. There is no buzz quite like that of a large City dealing room on a busy day. It is a truly extraordinary place, where intense competitive pressure combines with huge rewards and massive risks, both personal and professional. It gave me the financial independence to leave by the age of forty, but it cost me a marriage. I experienced tremendous comradeship, but I also witnessed ferocious politicking, immense greed and the bitterness of disappointment. It is a place where people are not always at their best.

I have tried to capture some of these qualities in the characters and incidents I have written about. They are all fictitious, but draw on the experiences of a key part of my life. Please do not feel sorry for the characters who come to grief. Like gamblers in a casino, they know the risks and make their own decisions – and they do not complain when they win.

They are not all bad either. There are still those – few in number – who take the City on their own terms, keep their distance and remain intact. I count many of my own former colleagues among their number. I look back on my twelve years in the City with a sense of nostalgia. I will always miss it, but I am pleased to have drawn a line when I did.

✥ DIARY ✥

0415 hrs. My driver drops me at home. It's been a long day in the City. First we had dinner at Orso's, then on to Stringfellow's and finally Ali's Bar. I'm mentally exhausted and emotionally drained. I run for the bathroom, trying not to wake my wife.

0430 hrs. After I've cleaned up I quietly enter the bedroom, remove my jacket and tie and start to undo my trousers. My wife stirs, looks up and puts the light on. *Fuck.* 'Early start,' I lie. '6 a.m. conference call with Tokyo.' I re-zip my trousers, retie my tie, put my jacket on and head back downstairs. I'm still too drunk to drive so I call a cab.

0545 hrs. Alone in the office with nothing to do, head still fuzzy, feeling ill. I try to remember who I was with last night and what I might have done or said. I find some big Amex slips in my pocket. Better remember to charge them to a client account. *Fuck.* I need to slow down. This could get out of hand.

0615 hrs. I'm so bored I start going through other people's desks. Nothing. Boring bastards. Or maybe they're just too smart. On the other hand, we don't attract the brightest things on two legs at Société Financière de Paris, so maybe I was right the first time. I try to play computer games to while away the time, but I start to feel sick.

0830 hrs. Must have fallen asleep. The phones are ringing but none of the team are here. Can't complain. I don't go in for macho face-time in the office and don't expect the team to either. Let the fucking phones ring.

0855 hrs. One phone keeps ringing. Should I answer it? I finally summon the determination and hit the button at the second attempt. 'SFP,' I bark aggressively. The caller hangs up. This freaks me out. Who the fuck rings up at five to nine in the morning, lets the phone ring and ring and then hangs up when you answer? Could be some bastard checking up on me. *Fuck.* Better watch out.

0930 hrs. The team have finally started to drift in. They're all hung over. Somebody says it was my fault for insisting on them all attending birthday drinks for Samantha at *The Avenue*. Who the fuck is Samantha? Apparently the blonde temp with the big personality who was with us last week. I'd forgotten about *The Avenue*.

0945 hrs. They're all here now, the lazy bastards. One or two look very ill. At least they made the effort. I cancel the morning meeting.

1015 hrs. My secretary brings me a coffee in my office, remarks it seems stuffy, would I mind if she turns up the air-conditioning? *Fuck.* I go out to Pink's and buy a clean shirt and underwear, then on to Boots for a shaving kit, and disappear to the directors' washroom. When I get back, she says it seems cooler now, perhaps she should turn the air-con back down. I settle down to read the paper.

1130 hrs. Weekly directors' meeting. I make sure I'm early, so that I can sit close to Simon, though not too close in case he thinks the air-conditioning needs turning up too. I make a big thing about the Client Marketing Initiative that I'm leading on at group level for the division. It's all bullshit, no one believes in it, but they all wait for Simon's reaction and then nod vigorously when he seems to agree. Phew, made it for another week.

1230 hrs. Christ, I need a drink. Thank God, I've got lunch today with Jimmy Smith from Swiss Credit. He knows how to have lunch. I take a cab to the City Club.

1530 hrs. Hallelujah! Saved. I feel warm, relaxed, at ease again. That was a freakish morning. I'm tired, but at least I've rejoined the human race. Back at my desk I fire off some e-mails about the Client Marketing Initiative, the need for cross-marketing on a multi-product, inter-divisional basis if we are to compete with the Americans, the lessons to be drawn from recent marketing failures, and suggest it's all reviewed at an off-site – where? – yes, brilliant! – in South Africa in April. Simon's half South African and I know he'll kill for a chance to be down there for the rugby. A fine afternoon's work. My secretary brings me my *Sporting Life* and I get down to serious business, just in time for the four o'clock from Sandown.

1630 hrs. Review time. Two of the graduate trainees have completed their probationary period in the department. Edwards is a spotty creep with a PhD and a high opinion of himself. Works damned hard and doesn't always come out for a drink when I summon the team to drink with me. Diane on the other hand is a darling, incredibly cute, something of a flirt, sends me the most outrageous e-mails. I extend his probationary period for another six months; he almost bursts into tears. I nearly lose it, try desperately to think of terminal illnesses, bankruptcy, losing my car parking space underneath the building, anything not to laugh. I tell Diane she has made it. She is overwhelmed, agrees to dinner to review her career options and how far she might go from here. Must think carefully how I play that one.

1745 hrs. Simon wants to do the off-site in South Africa.

He wants me to lead on it, sends an e-mail to all the directors, urging full co-operation in this important initiative. I instruct the whole team to work on an agenda and a presentation for me to give. I want it ready for the morning, so that I can show it to Simon. Then I head off to meet Adam Whitehead from Hellerbank for drinks.

1930 hrs. Three Martinis later and I'm flying again. I try to recall what I told my wife about this evening. *Fuck.* Did I tell her anything? Did she tell me anything? *Fuck.*

2250 hrs. I'm lost. Staggered out of dinner and caught a cab, but threw up in the back and the driver ordered me out. *Fuck.*

0130 hrs. I'm trying to work out how to use my mobile. It isn't normally this hard. *Fuck.* I push a button. I hear a vaguely familiar voice. 'Taxi desk, please.' Then the voice starts shouting at me, 'For God's sake – it's me! Where the hell are you? We were due at the Evans's for supper at 8:00. I've been calling you all evening. No-one knows where you are.' *Fuck.* I've got to slow down. One of these days this could get out of hand.

✦ DINNER PARTY ✦

'Richard, how good to see you!'

'Lucy, darling – as gorgeous as ever! I'm so sorry I'm so late – I got stuck in the office. Here, these are for you.'

He handed her an enormous bunch of lilies selected by his secretary and gave her a peck on the cheek. She showed him into the dining room.

'Everybody, I'd like you to meet one of my oldest friends – Richard was at Oxford with me, but now he's a partner at Hardman Stoney, the American investment bank in the City. Richard, this is Gavin and his wife Sheila. Gavin writes for *The Guardian*, and Sheila's a full-time mum! And this is Arthur, who works with me in the library at the LSE, and his partner Josh, who's in therapy. Josh is a super-duper cook and he's prepared the pudding tonight. And this is Alison. Alison works for the probation service.'

Richard nodded and shook hands and said hello and asked himself for the thousandth time why, in a moment of insane weakness, he had ever agreed to come to dinner. And why, for God's sake, hadn't he cancelled? Partners of Hardman Stoney were notorious for their social *faux pas*, turning up on social occasions late or not at all. Why hadn't he simply cancelled?

In part, he supposed, it was curiosity. Once upon a time, Lucy and he had briefly been an item, and he was curious to know how she had fared in the years that had passed. She looked older now, and dowdy, and he wondered where her earlier beauty had gone. Perhaps it had never been there in the first place. Her house in Hackney was tiny and shabby and was in a part of town that he had never visited before. He felt distinctly over-dressed in the company of her friends. He was in a double-breasted, pinstriped suit, complete with Hermès tie and Patek Philippe watch, and they

13

were in corduroys, denims, open shirts and rolled-up sleeves. Josh was smoking what appeared to be a joint. Richard took it all in, but said nothing. They were all looking at him.

'I'm sorry to be so late. I got stuck in the office.' He shrugged. They looked at him blankly.

Lucy intervened. 'Don't worry, I kept you a plate of pasta, and Josh doesn't mind holding the pudding while you eat, do you, Josh, darling?'

Josh ignored her and carried on staring at Richard.

The pasta was half cold, stodgy and almost tasteless. He ploughed his way through it in silence. Lucy could feel the tension.

'So Richard, why don't you tell us all about your work? It must be wonderful, flying all over the world at the drop of a hat, Concorde to New York, trips to Hong Kong, Tokyo, Frankfurt…'

'It's okay. It's not as glamorous as people think.'

'Oh really?' It was Josh. 'The last time I flew Concorde I thought it was terribly glam. What did everybody else think?'

They all laughed.

'Everybody, please, this is so unfair.' Lucy was concerned for her guest. 'It's no use you all ganging up on Richard just because he's rich and talented and successful. It's not your fault you earn such mega-bonuses, is it, darling?' she said, touching him playfully on the knee.

He smiled, uncertain how to respond, wishing he was somewhere – anywhere – else. It was clear that Lucy had been drinking, but he wondered if they had all been smoking joints.

'So how much do you earn, Richard?' It was Alison, the probation officer. He looked at her, taking in the barely concealed hostility. To hell with it, he thought, why should we always be on the receiving end?

'Oh, in an average year about the same as two hundred probation officers, I suppose – assuming they all get performance bonuses, of course. I am right in thinking you're eligible for £500 annual performance incentives, aren't I?'

She sat back in her chair and almost hissed at him.

He looked thoughtful. 'That means, with sixty partners in the London office…' he paused, reached into his jacket pocket and pulled out a calculator, into which he tapped some numbers, '…we could cover the salaries of twelve thousand probation officers for a year. Interesting, isn't it? How many probation officers are there in the service as a whole?'

Before she could answer, Josh came through from the kitchen, carrying dessert.

'How wonderful!' beamed Lucy, seizing on the distraction. 'Look, everybody, isn't Josh brilliant?'

She kissed Josh on the cheek and Alison subsided into silence. Sheila turned to Richard.

'What exactly do you do, Richard?'

He paused to collect his thoughts while Josh handed round the crème brulée.

'Well, I buy businesses. Not for our clients, you understand, for ourselves. I act as principal, not as an adviser to other people.'

Alison looked up. 'Principle? Did you say principle? That's a laugh.'

'No, Alison,' he smiled as patronisingly as he could. 'Principal.' He emphasised the last syllable as strongly as he could. 'There's a very important difference. Principals can act without having regard to principles, always providing they don't actually break the law or do anything that would bring the firm into disrepute. Our principle is to maximise returns for the firm. We buy businesses, put in new management, strip out costs, then sell them on for a profit. Our principle is the principle of enlightened self-interest. Didn't

15

you ever see the movie 'Wall Street'? Do you remember that great Michael Douglas speech – 'Greed is good'…or is it 'God'? – I can never remember!'

He helped himself to a large spoonful of dessert. 'Mmm…this is excellent. Well done, Josh!'

He could feel them scowling at him, though Lucy tried to keep the conversation going, desperately hoping to salvage the evening.

'But Richard, you still haven't really explained to those of us who don't work in the City what your job actually involves from day to day?'

'He strips out costs,' interrupted Gavin. 'It means he fires people to increase profits.'

Richard looked at Gavin, weighing him up carefully. He had to be careful, he was starting to enjoy himself too much. He took a sip of wine and tried not to grimace. He checked the bottle, which was standing on the sideboard. It brought back memories of student days.

'Well, technically speaking that's not quite right. A business might have any amount of underutilised assets tied up in it – buildings, land, plant and machinery, for example…and of course people. What we try to do is slim the business down so that it's as efficient as possible. We take a long hard look at it, get out our calculators, and do what's commercially expedient.'

Gavin threw down his spoon.

'Oh, God – I don't believe it! You City people make me sick. Do you ever think of the social consequences of what you do? If you 'slim down' a factory, let's say in a small town in the north-east, where there's high unemployment, what do those people actually do? Do you have any idea what high unemployment does to divorce rates? Do you know what happens to suicides? Or mental illness? Or drug and alcohol abuse? Or crime? Or child abuse? Well, do you?!'

Richard stared at him, wide-eyed, his eyes suddenly

opened by Gavin's revelation. It was time to go. If he did not leave now, this would definitely get physical.

'Gavin, you're quite right! I've never seen it that way before, but you're so, so right. How can I have been so blind?' He turned to Lucy. 'Lucy, I'm so sorry, but I have to go. I have to get back to the office. I need to get this stuff down on paper. Thank you for a wonderful evening.' He kissed her on the cheek and turned to Josh. 'And Josh, the dessert was superb, you're a star.' He leant forward and kissed Josh on the cheek. Josh scowled back at him. 'But what Gavin's said demands action. Hardman Stoney has a whole stack of investments in the north-east, seven companies, if I'm not mistaken, and I've never really thought about them in the way Gavin described tonight.' He turned to Gavin. 'Gavin, you're absolutely right. Those small towns must be hotbeds of social upheaval, crime, drug abuse, what did you say – oh yes, alcohol abuse,' he looked at Alison, 'wife beating. In fact it's clear to me that those places simply aren't suitable for us to be doing business in.' They were staring at him, baffled. 'From now on, I'll ensure that we hold the Annual General Meetings of all those businesses down here in London. Management committees too. It'll save on travel costs, and will mean we don't have to risk going up there.' He reached across the table and slapped Gavin on the shoulder, before heading for the door. 'Lucy – thanks again. Gavin – thanks for the insight – the less my team and I see of those places in future, the happier we shall be!' He winked and closed the door a split second before Gavin's wine glass smashed into it.

⚜ TEAM MOVE ⚜

£1 million a year, guaranteed for three years.'

'Jesus Christ! You've got my attention.'

She could not help smiling, and sat back in her chair, taking a moment to sip her wine. She had deliberately insisted on a corner table where they could not be overheard. She had been nervous approaching Mark, her deputy, in case it backfired. If he went running off to tell the board, she would be in deep water.

'You'd still be my number two, but you'd join as a managing director on a base salary of a hundred and thirty. All the usual perks, plus I told them they'd have to give you the car of your choice, knowing what a speed freak you are.'

He laughed.

'Are you serious? Any car?'

'Well, within reason. I specifically mentioned the new 911, and they said it wouldn't be a problem.'

He looked at her curiously.

'How long have you been planning this?'

It was her turn to laugh.

'They first approached me through a headhunter six months ago. I played hard to get, but I soon realised they were serious. Bartons don't have a Convertible team at all, and we're one of the top three teams in the City by pretty much any measure. But I couldn't do it on my own. I need you, and I need most of the rest of the team.'

'A team move? They want to lift the whole team?'

She nodded.

'Lock, stock and barrel. They'll take everyone we think we need.'

'Okay, so how do we do it?'

She paused. This was the tricky bit.

'Well, I won't pretend it'll be easy. And I'm counting on

you to play a pivotal role. The difficulty I face is that as a managing director my legal and contractual responsibilities are much more onerous than yours. If I act against the firm's best interests, they can nail me. And to be frank I have a higher profile. You're in a much better position. And the team look to you for day-to-day leadership. You hired most of them before I even joined the firm. Sure, they respect me, but I was just the hotshot the firm brought in to stir things up. You'd been there for almost five years before I even started. Do you feel up to it?'

He paused, looking pensive. Oh God, she thought to herself, I hope I haven't blown it.

He nodded.

'Sure. I can do it.'

He called across to the waiter, indicating his empty gin and tonic glass.

'Waiter – mine's a large one!'

She had heard him say that a dozen times before, and laughed now with relief as much as genuine humour.

'Well it would be, wouldn't it? Now, let's think who to approach first.'

They met again a few days later. She would not discuss it at all in the office, and was paranoid about the lawsuits that would surely fly if it leaked.

'How's it going?'

He laughed.

'So far, it's easy. Jack, Nico and Ben are on board. All three will need guarantees, but two years will be fine. Ben will have to go up to senior manager. I said we'd raise their base salaries by twenty per cent. I'm waiting to hear back from Sandy.'

'Brilliant, well done! Any problems with Sandy?'

'There won't be once I tell him the rest of us are off to Bartons whatever he decides.'

'Okay, keep me posted. What else do we need to worry about?'

'I want to see my offer letter from Bartons. I can't take the risk of resigning without it.'

'I know, leave it to me. Let's get together again on Monday night.'

She sat in the corner worrying, checking and rechecking her watch. He arrived fifteen minutes late, breathless.

'Sorry, got held up. I was chatting to Roger.'

'Any problems?'

'None at all, it's sweet as can be. Sandy, Ian and Martin are on board. Roger, too, I think, but he wants to sleep on it overnight.'

'Have you got the numbers?'

'Sure – here.'

He handed over a list of what he had agreed with the team. Against each name was a title and job description, base salary and guaranteed bonus number, with either a two or a three against it to indicate the number of years that would be guaranteed. She glanced down the list. For a moment he looked concerned.

'It's a lot, but it's right for the team.'

She smiled, looking at the totals at the bottom of the list.

'Don't worry, it's well within budget. If we can do this so cheaply we may have to look again at our own packages.'

He looked at her, hesitated and then asked, 'What is your package?'

She looked surprised, and he thought he saw the faintest hint of a blush.

'Mark, I can't tell you that. It wouldn't be right. I shall still be your boss, after all.'

'I know, but I feel right now as if I'm the one taking all the risks. I feel as if I should be more like your partner in all this than your number two.'

'Mark, let's get something straight. I'm the boss. You're my number two. An important number two, but still number two. I've got you a fabulous package. Think what you'll be able to do with that kind of money. If you're not sure you want to do this, say so now.'

'Of course I still want to do it, but you forget I'm having all these conversations and I haven't even seen my offer letter yet.'

'Leave that with me. I'm on the case.'

Over a week passed before they met again.

'What's going on? Why the delay? We're losing momentum and I need those offer letters to give to the team. Doing things this way is fine, but if the guys are expected to come in on our coat-tails without even having interviews with the Bartons people, then they need those letters. Where are they?'

'Relax. I've got them. Well, almost all of them. Here.'

She passed a stack of envelopes across the table. He leafed through them and looked up at her.

'Where's mine?'

'Ours are both delayed. It's nothing to worry about. Because we're joining as MDs our appointments have to be blessed by their senior appointments board. It's a formality. We'll have ours by the end of the week.'

He looked her in the eye.

'Jane, just how certain are you of this? Once I start handing these out, the team will go ahead and resign, and we could be hung out to dry.'

She laughed.

'Look, I've met the guys from Bartons. They're serious people, long-term, heavyweight, they don't dick people about. You distribute the letters to the team, and I tell you what, I'll resign anyway, even without my offer letter. You go in after me.'

He looked at her.

'Okay, it's a risk, but let's do it.'

He raised his glass to her.

'Success!'

'Wealth!'

The chairman's office was on the twentieth floor, with a spectacular view across the City to St. Paul's. She took a deep breath, knocked and entered.

'Ah, Miss Leach. How are things on the Convertible desk?'

'Very good, thank you, Sir Arnold.'

She was surprised to see Mike Hatchett, the Group Legal Adviser, sitting in the corner.

'Sir Arnold, I wanted to have a word with you, preferably in private, if I may.'

'By all means, my dear, but first I have something to say to you.'

She was startled.

'I'm afraid, my dear, I have bad news for you. I'm having to let you go. You see, you've been rather naughty, haven't you?'

She swallowed. What did he know? Who had leaked it? She had no choice now, she was committed. She would have to carry on regardless.

'Sir Arnold, I don't know what you're talking about. But I may as well say to you what I intended anyway. I'm resigning. I have here a formal letter of resignation.'

She placed an envelope on his desk. He looked at her and, without opening the envelope, picked it up and dropped it in the bin by the desk.

'No, my dear, you're not resigning. I'm dismissing you from the firm for cause. Effective immediately. Mike has an envelope for you here, outlining the legal and financial implications of the termination of your employment.

Obviously you lose your stock options, your unvested shares, and your pension rights. I'm afraid you tried to be too clever. And that doesn't always pay, you know.'

She heard the door opening behind her and turned to see who had entered.

'Mark! What are you doing here? I haven't finished yet.'

Mark was smiling.

'I think you are finished, Jane. I think you're completely finished. You see, the team aren't going anywhere. You played a stupid, dumb, greedy game. I never rated you from the moment you arrived, and I don't rate you now. You wanted me to poach you a team, and then you would have hung me out to dry. Left me behind. Well, I'm not as stupid as you think.' He looked towards Sir Arnold. 'I value loyalty, and so does this firm. I don't need to move to Bartons to get a world-class package, and neither do the team.'

'Not at all,' said Sir Arnold, moving to stand beside Mark and put his arm around his shoulder. 'We have a world-class Convertible team, and we're very proud of them. A pay rise has been long overdue and I'm very happy to sanction it.' He beamed at Mark.

She gasped, feeling a rush of blood to the head. She reached inside her handbag and pulled out a piece of paper.

'Here! Look at this list. Your blue-eyed boy wrote out a list of all the people in the team with packages, guarantees, the works!'

'I know he did,' said Sir Arnold. 'And I know exactly how you came by it.'

He walked over to his desk, opened a drawer and took out a folder. He pulled out an identical list from the folder.

'This is the list that I commissioned Mark to produce. I needed to know exactly what was necessary to keep the team. That, and the knowledge that your previous share of the bonus pool would be prorated around them. Really, my dear. You don't think we were born yesterday, do you?'

Mark smiled.

'Don't worry, Jane – I'm sure it was really you that Bartons were after, and not the team. Mind you, without a team, you might have to do some of the work yourself.' He laughed. 'I'm sure you'll cope.'

✣ INFATUATION ✣

From: Alex Spears
Sent: 27 March 2002 08:11
To: Julia Peters
Subject: Last night
How are you? I guess we all had a bit too much to drink last night. I'm feeling gruesome this morning. I feel like I made a bit of a fool of myself, but these things have a way of happening to me. For what it's worth, I meant what I said, and I'd love to see you again, if you feel up to it. There's a new wine bar on the Fulham Road called Lomo's – it's not far from your place and I've heard it's really cool. Let me know if you fancy meeting up there one evening.
Regards,
Alex

From: Julia Peters
Sent: 27 March 2002 11:37
To: Alex Spears
Subject: Re Last night
I'm fine. I guess I was a bit surprised, that's all. Those vodka shots didn't help. My head's killing me. I'd like to meet up again, but just for a drink. Let's try to take it easy. I feel kind of weird about the whole thing, what with you being head of the team and a managing director. I've heard of Lomo's – it sounds good, but definitely NO MORE VODKA!!!!
Regards,
Julia

From: Alex Spears
Sent: 27 March 2002 11:49

To: Julia Peters
Subject: Re Re Last night .
Fantastic! Does tomorrow evening work for you? I'll make sure you're not on lates. How about 7 o'clock sharp at Lomo's?
Regards,
Alex

From: Julia Peters
Sent: 4 April 2002 08:50
To: Alex Spears
Subject: Wow!
How are you? Last night was amazing. I'm sitting here blushing just thinking about it. I still feel kind of weird, but wonderful at the same time. Has anyone ever told you you're amazing?!!!!!!
Julia
xxxxxx

From: Alex Spears
Sent: 4 April 2002 09:05
To: Julia Peters
Subject: Re Wow!
Now I'm the one trying not to blush. I keep wanting to look at you and grin! You don't know how hard it is for me with you sitting just twenty feet away. Open-plan offices are great, but sometimes I just wish I could shut myself away somewhere. You were WICKED last night. I'm so glad we got together. Don't change!!!
Luv, Alex
xxxxxxxx
PS What are you doing tonight?

From: Julia Peters
Sent: 4 April 2002 09:11
To: Alex Spears

Subject: Re Re Wow!
I hope what I'm doing is seeing my lover. I can't wait to get out of here tonight. Time just seems to drag and d – r – a – g. Where shall we eat? Or shall I cook for you? My mother says I do the finest beef Wellington in the western world. Would you like me to cook for you?
Love and hugs,
Julia
xxxxxxx

From: Alex Spears
Sent: 4 April 2002 09:15
To: Julia Peters
Subject: Re Re Re Wow!
Whoa girl! Cooking sounds great, but I can cook too, you know, and too much beef Wellington will have me looking like a sumo wrestler. And I don't think you'd like that, would you? I wouldn't want to squash you – well, maybe a little! I'll have to catch you later. I've got to go upstairs to the MDs' weekly bullshit session.
Seeyalater.
Alex
Xxxxxxx

From: Julia Peters
Sent: 19 April 2002 08:20
To: Alex Spears
Subject: That was cool
Alex darling, that was fun, fun, fun! I love your house. You are soooooo lucky. And so am I. And Gordon Ramsay is a great restaurant. But did you see how the waiter looked when I kissed you? I know you still feel self-conscious, but I DON'T. I feel great. I'm in love and I'm proud of it, and I don't care if the whole world knows – even if my lover-boss is terrified of finding a

client or some stupid colleague sitting at the next table! Imagine if it was Sir Oliver? He'd be so shocked!!!!! I want to stay at your house again. It felt as if we were a real couple, we could just be ourselves without worrying about other people. Tell me you love me and want to hold me tight.

Love,

Julia

xxxxxxxxxxxx

From: Alex Spears
Sent: 19 April 2002 08:51
To: Julia Peters
Subject: Re That was cool

Julia my darling, you don't know how good it feels to see those words from you. If you knew some of the things I've been through – anyway, enough of all that. One of these days I'll tell you the whole gruesome tale. The main thing is that was the past and this is the present. I DO feel self-conscious at times, but you forget I'm fifteen years older than you. I was more of a free spirit once, but we older hands have learnt that it pays to be careful. I'm glad you liked the restaurant, and delighted you like the house. I gave it a total make-over after my divorce, trying to wipe out the memories. And it was good to wake up together. I watched you while you were asleep. You are truly wonderful and I adore you.

Lots of love,

Alex

XXXXXXXXXXXXXXXXXXXX

From: Julia Peters
Sent: 2 May 2002 08:02
To: Alex Spears
Subject: I missed you

Welcome back! The last week's been too awful for

words. While you were gadding off to Tokyo I just had the most miserable time imaginable. If only I could have come with you. I was so unhappy. I just wanted to be with you and for you to hold me.

Anyway, it's confession time. I told mummy and daddy about you. I know you asked me not to, but it's so hard not being able to talk to anyone. I'm sure some of the girls here suspect, but I don't care. Anyway, when I explained who you are, they gave me such a terrible time. Mummy cried. Daddy was upset and wouldn't look me in the eye. I said you're an MD and you'll look after me, and I told them how I love you. They wouldn't speak to me. I'm so confused, I just feel like bursting into tears the whole time.

Love,

Julia

xxxxxxxxxxx

From: Alex Spears
Sent: 2 May 2002 08:08
To: Julia Peters
Subject: Re I missed you

I missed you too, my darling! It was just impossible to call you when I wanted to, what with the time difference and my meeting schedule and the people from the Tokyo office always hanging around. I left you messages, but I kept missing you. My bed felt empty at night – what more can I say? I'm sorry to hear about your parents, but it doesn't surprise me. We'll just have to grit our teeth and see it through. Perhaps I should meet them, try to put their minds at rest. When they see how happy we are together, they'll come round. Chin up – we'll tough it out together.

Lots of love,

Alex

XXXXXXXXXXXXXXXXXXX

From: Alex Spears
Sent: 15 May 2002 08:17
To: Julia Peters
Subject: Where were you last night?

My darling, what happened last night? I waited up for you until 2 a.m. Your mobile was switched off all evening. I went round to your old flat but you weren't there. I even tried Lomo's, but they hadn't seen you either. Where were you? I know you've been upset lately, but things will be fine – believe me. For starters I'm going to get you promoted in June, it's virtually signed and sealed, and you won't believe the pay rise. And I've thought again about Bali – let's just do it! Who cares if half the City are there? Please talk to me. We need to communicate. If we can't communicate we're nothing. We need to share things with each other, lean on each other for help when we're down. You look tired today. I just want to come over to you and hug you and kiss you. PLEASE talk to me!

All my love forever,

Alex

XXXXXXXXXXXXXXXXXXXXXXXXXXXXXXXXX X

From: Julia Peters
Sent: 15 May 2002 11:35
To: Alex Spears
Subject: Re Where were you last night?

Alex, I'm sorry, but I needed some space. I went home to mummy and daddy and spent the night there. I haven't slept. I couldn't sleep, with all that's on my mind. They were very good, and they did finally listen to me. But I've come to a decision and you're not going to like it. We have to stop seeing each other. I've thought long and hard about this, and I'm not saying it lightly. It's been great, truly it has, but it's not for me.

I've never loved another woman before, Alex, and you opened my eyes. But I'm not a lesbian, I'm just confused, insecure and out of my depth. I'll never forget you. Please don't call me again.

Regards,

Julia

PS Daddy says he's writing to Sir Oliver. He's angry and spiteful and I just think he wants to hurt you. He says he's going to tell Sir Oliver how you seduced me. I told him it didn't feel like seduction at the time, but I don't know now. I'm so confused. I hope this doesn't ruin your career, truly I do. I know how much it matters to you to be the first woman MD at Bartons. If I can help at all you know you can count on me. Please forgive me. I hope that when the dust has settled we can still be friends.

✦ SMART PEOPLE ✦

Karl looked around the room. There was an almost palpable feeling of tension. The other candidates were trying to appear calm, but gave the game away by constantly taking surreptitious glances at each other, weighing up the competition. There were three of them – two men and a woman. All were wearing what they thought would best pass for business attire. Jason, from Manchester, was in his only suit, a light blue wool and polyester mix from M & S. Paul, from Dublin, was in a heavy dark pinstripe, pure wool, but undoubtedly borrowed, given away by the baggy fit of the jacket. Linda, from Essex, was in what some glossy magazine had probably told her was the latest 'City girl' power suit.

Karl relaxed. They were children. He would walk this interview. After their initial mutual introductions, conversation had become increasingly stilted and had finally dried up. It was well known that the Mergers and Acquisitions Department of Bartons only took on two 'exceptional' graduate trainees each year. They preferred to hire people with professional qualifications such as accountants and lawyers, or in extremis MBAs.

Karl's Brooks Brothers suit was expensive – by his usual standards it had cost a small fortune – but his uncle, who was a senior banker at Schleppenheimer in New York, had offered to pick up the tab if he got the job. His tie was Hermès, a staggeringly expensive extravagance for a student, but one which he saw as an investment. His slicked-down fair hair was his own idea. Karl took a deep breath. He felt as well prepared as he could possibly be. He had been given a checklist by his uncle and was nothing if not diligent. He looked around again at the other candidates, and wondered maliciously if he should try to give himself an extra edge – after all, it was not just about being good, but about being better than the others. He cleared his throat.

'What did you think of the non-farm payroll numbers in the US last night?'

He was looking at Jason, but his question could have been aimed at any of them. Jason gulped and blushed, staring guppy-like at Karl.

'You did see them?' asked Karl with mock seriousness.

'N – no...'

Karl put his hand to his head in astonishment.

'Oh, for God's sake. These guys are professionals. They take the whole process seriously and they expect us to as well. Presumably you're at least up to date with the internal reorganisation at Bartons? There was an excellent account of it in this week's *Capital Markets Review*.'

Now they were all doing guppy impressions. He almost laughed.

'And you must have read Sir Oliver Barton's speech at Davos about the future of international investment banking? It's been on the Barton's web-site for the past three weeks.'

They looked utterly shocked, appalled, in fact stark naked. It was very hard not to grin.

'Come on, guys. This firm wants people who can *think*.'

He stared around the room at them.

'Oh well,' he shrugged. 'I don't suppose it will matter.'

Before any of them could reply, the door opened and a smiling secretary entered.

'Mister Koenig?'

She looked around the candidates and smiled as Karl nodded and stood up.

'Mister Butcher will see you now.'

Karl smiled and went to follow her out of the room. As the door was about to close behind him, he could not resist turning to grin smugly at his fellow candidates.

'Good luck, guys!' he said as the door closed behind him. No one spoke. They looked helplessly at one another.

'Come in, Mister Koenig.'

The door swung silently shut behind Karl. He was in an enormous corner office with vast floor-to-ceiling windows looking out over the City. At one end, some thirty feet away, was a huge desk with a big leather swivel chair behind it. Some ten feet in front of the desk was a small metal frame chair, standing alone in the middle of the room. It looked more like the scene for an interrogation than an interview. Butcher himself was an enormous bear of a man, probably in his forties, very tall with a thick mane of dark hair, receding at the temples. He was in his shirtsleeves, standing behind his desk with his tie undone, a chunky Rolex on his wrist. He looked more like a boxer than a banker.

Karl stepped forward and walked self-consciously towards the desk to shake hands.

'Stop!'

Butcher's voice boomed out as Karl passed the small metal-framed chair. He wiped his hands nervously down the sides of his trousers, a trick his uncle had taught him – there was apparently nothing worse than a limp, wet handshake.

'Mister Koenig, I take it you are aware that the programme you are seeking to join is one of the most highly sought-after entry-level positions in the City?'

'Yes…sir,' replied Karl. He was not sure why he had added the 'sir', but it seemed the right thing to do in the face of Butcher's booming authority.

'Mister Koenig – what do you think are the key qualities we are seeking in the young people we hire?'

Karl was flustered. This was not what he had expected.

'Er…well…I suppose intelligence, hard work and commitment.'

Butcher looked at him but did not react.

'Mister Koenig!'

'Yes sir?'

'Mister Koenig – do you see that chair beside you?'

Karl looked at the chair.

'Yes, sir.'

'Mister Koenig, I want you to climb onto that chair and stand on it.'

Karl was baffled. This was all going terribly wrong. What on earth was he supposed to do now? He swallowed hard and stepped up onto the chair, standing with his arms by his sides, looking pitifully towards Butcher. The seconds passed as Butcher stared at him. He could feel his pulse racing in his head and wondered what this was meant to prove.

'Thank you, Mister Koenig. You may get down now.'

Karl stepped down and stood uncertainly, wondering what to do next. Butcher had written something on a form on his desk. Now he looked up at Karl.

'Thank you. You may leave.'

Karl was totally bewildered.

'Is that all…sir?'

Butcher looked at him, apparently surprised that he had not already left.

'Of course that's all, Mister Koenig. You don't think we have a place for you at Bartons, do you? We need people who are prepared to question what others take for granted. We don't want people who just take orders. We want people who can think, Mister Koenig – people who can *think*!'

Karl felt as if the floor was about to swallow him up. He half turned towards the door, desperately trying to find something to say. His desperate mental fumblings were interrupted by Butcher's booming voice.

'You have a lot to learn, Mister Koenig, not least being how to think. Now, how about starting by *thinking* your way to the door? I have other candidates to see!'

All eyes turned to him as he stepped out of Butcher's office. He looked pale. It was Jason who spoke first.

'That was quick. Are you all right?'

Karl turned and looked at him. Should he help them? Should he explain what would happen to them? It was irrelevant as far as he was concerned – he had already blown it. But would they believe him if he did tell them? He thought for a moment and smiled smugly.

'No problem at all – it was great. And guys – one tip from me. Whatever happens, *don't* stand on the chair.'

⚜ TAKEOVER ⚜

For once, people were early for the weekly directors' meeting. Rupert noted with satisfaction that even some of the poorer attenders were present, people who showed their faces once or twice a year, if at all.

'Gentlemen,' he said, attempting to call the meeting to order. The low murmur of conversation continued, as numerous side conversations carried on while he tried to get the meeting under way. It seemed to him there was a hostile undercurrent. Typical, he thought. 'Gentlemen, today is a very important day for us. As you know, the acquisition of the firm by Schweizerische Grossbank went unconditional on Tuesday.' He looked around the table to see who was paying attention. ' We now have new owners.' Still, a low buzz continued. He hoped the faces around the table understood the full import of what he was saying. 'Gentlemen, as a sign of their immediate commitment to the business, and an early indication of how serious they are about understanding what it is that we all do here in London, SGB have sent Ernst Fleischfresser over from Zurich. Dr Fleischfresser is one of the most senior members of the SGB board, and has been charged with developing their international strategy. He had dinner with Sir Colin last night to talk about the integration of the Asset Management business and today he's devoting himself to meetings with key personnel in the various Investment Banking Departments.' He looked around meaningfully. 'Starting with us in Corporate Finance.' For the first time there was silence around the table. 'I've invited him to join this meeting so that he can get a flavour of the department, who the directors are, and what sort of projects we're all pursuing. Anne will bring him in shortly to join us. Are there any questions?'

For a moment the silence continued, then half a dozen people tried to speak at once.

'One at a time, please,' said Rupert, pleased to have the chance for once to exert some authority. 'Paul, would you like to kick off?'

'I certainly would.' Paul Rowntree was one of the older directors, a dinosaur who had been with the firm for over twenty-five years. He had one or two 'special relationships' on the corporate side, though he had not produced a meaningful fee from them in the last five years. But he was abrasive, forceful and had been a major shareholder in the firm before the takeover. 'Rupert, what in hell went on in those final negotiations? The price SGB are paying is barely enough to cover the value of our Asset Management business, let alone the rest of the firm.' There were murmurs of agreement around the table. 'It's as if we've sold Asset Management for no premium and thrown in the rest of the firm for free. What's going on?'

Rupert stared at the older man. 'Look, Paul, what's done is done. The terms have been agreed and announced. They're final. What do you hope to achieve by raking over old coals now?'

Rowntree leant forward aggressively. 'Rupert, I don't want to call into question your wisdom or...' he coughed ostentatiously, '...authority in this meeting, but I would like to know who was involved from our side in negotiating the terms.' He leant back in his chair and folded his arms, having thrown down the gauntlet to Rupert.

Rupert looked wretched, blushed scarlet and looked around the room, out of the windows, down at his papers, anywhere but at Rowntree.

'Well, if you must know...Sir Colin decided to negotiate the final stages himself.'

Rowntree leant forward, incredulous. 'So are you saying that no director from Corporate Finance was involved in the final stages of a transaction in which our own firm was sold?'

'Yes!' Rupert was almost tearful. 'Yes, dammit. And right now our new lord and master is sitting fifty yards away down the corridor in my office, waiting to be summoned here to meet us all. So let's stop raking over the coals and start thinking what we're going to say to him, shall we?'

The faces round the table were ashen. Rowntree, square-jawed and belligerent, gave Rupert an unforgiving, hostile stare.

'So what you're saying, Rupert, is that the final stages were delegated upwards from the people in this firm who are meant to be experts to someone who doesn't know his arse from his elbow when it comes to selling companies? The Swiss went over our heads until they reached a level of sufficient incompetence to be able to do the sort of deal they wanted.' He gazed around at his colleagues. 'And now you expect us all to be good boys, do as we're told, not rock the boat and WALK NAKED INTO THE GAS CHAMBER! Is that correct?'

Rupert felt near to breaking. 'Look, Paul, there's no point going into this now! Let's just think what we're going to say to Fleischfresser, shall we?'

Rowntree was icy as he contemplated the younger man, his head of department.

'I suppose we have to. It doesn't much matter for me, but there are people round this table, as well as elsewhere in the department, who have young families, mortgages, school fees, commitments. Don't you think your first priority should be to get our new owners to offer guarantees and lock-ins to key staff, so that we don't have a mass walkout of our most talented people?'

'I agree!' It was Charles Howard, a thirty-five-year-old considered one of the 'Young Turks' of the department. He was an old Etonian with impeccable social credentials, a man whose appearance was never short of crisp in a double-breasted old City sort of way. He turned and shouted to the room in general, 'Let's soak these Swiss bastards for all we can get!'

They cheered back enthusiastically, but then all heads turned as the door opened and a short, portly man in slacks and a dark brown check sports jacket entered, unannounced. He was wearing brown shoes and what seemed to be a polyester tie, bright red like a shop steward.

'Rupert, gentlemen, I'm sorry to interrupt.' He looked meaningfully at his watch. 'But I thought this meeting was meant to start promptly on the hour?' His English was heavily accented, guttural, and he gazed around the room, taking in the scene and focusing particularly on Howard.

'Dr Fleischfresser, welcome!' Rupert stood, blushing, and ushered the small Swiss into the room, pulling out the empty chair next to his own to allow him to sit down. 'Do sit down. Some coffee?'

Fleischfresser nodded. 'Cream and two sugars.'

'Oh, yes, of course.' Rupert looked around helplessly, until Howard reluctantly rose and went to the coffee pot and cups lined up at a side table.

'Now, Dr Fleischfresser, shall I do some introductions? Would it be helpful if I were to go around the table and introduce the directors in turn, and perhaps they could then say a few words about their particular clients and their current projects?'

'No.'

The temperature in the room fell by about five degrees. Rupert swallowed, feeling himself blushing again. Most of the others were staring down at their papers. Only Rowntree was fixing the Swiss with a malevolent stare.

Howard walked over to Fleischfresser carrying a fine bone china cup and saucer.

'Cream and two sugars, wasn't it, *Doktor* Fleischfresser?'

he asked silkily. He put the cup on the table in front of the Swiss. He looked at Rupert. 'Perhaps *Doktor* Fleischfresser would prefer to sit on the other side of the table, away from the radiator? It's less hot there.' As he turned to resume his seat, standing behind the Swiss where he could not be seen by their visitor, he gestured towards his polyester and wool mix jacket. Facing away from Fleischfresser, he half mumbled, 'His jacket might melt!' Several directors sitting nearby tried not to laugh, hiding their faces with their hands.

'Excuse me?' Fleischfresser turned to Howard. 'I missed what you said. Is there a problem?'

'Not at all, sir. Just let me know if you'd like a refill.'

Rupert's face was shiny with perspiration.

'Doktor Fleischfresser, we really would like to introduce ourselves to you properly. Are you sure that it wouldn't be helpful to go around the table?'

'Or for us to take turns under it?' muttered Howard as an aside.

Fleischfresser, who had again missed what Howard had said, turned towards him.

'What was that, Mister...?'

'Howard, sir. Charles Howard. I'm the youngest director in the department. I joined the firm straight from Balliol – that's an Oxford college,' he smiled condescendingly. 'So I have the privilege of serving the coffee.'

By way of reply, the Swiss picked up his coffee cup and noisily slurped from it, staring thoughtfully at Howard. Several of the directors again tried to hide their reactions, straining not to laugh. Only Rowntree openly rolled his eyes heavenwards.

Rupert took in the reactions around the table, realised it was potentially a decisive moment and dived in. He picked up his own coffee cup, raised it to his lips and slurped even more noisily than his guest. Fleischfresser, oblivious to the reaction around the table, turned angrily towards Rupert.

'What are you doing? Is this English humour?'

Rupert suffered a desperate panic attack and stared at the Swiss, his mouth open and his eyes bulging.

'Er…no…not at all.'

Fleischfresser pulled some papers from his jacket pocket.

'Gentlemen, I have here this department's results for the past three years.' He looked around the table, pausing for effect. 'They're terrible. Truly terrible. What have you got to say for yourselves?'

Dead silence. For what seemed like a very long time. Even Howard had stopped grinning, and Rowntree was suddenly focused on the Swiss in a less certain way.

'Gentlemen, I repeat – what have you got to say for yourselves?'

Rupert decided it was time to show some leadership.

'Dr Fleischfresser, I'm aware of our recent track record, but you must understand that three years is a very short time over which to judge the Corporate Finance Department. This is a long-term, relationship-driven business. Sometimes it can take many years for a corporate relationship to bear fruit. We've always taken comfort from the fact that, in the end, we're always there. We have a long-term approach.'

Fleischfresser turned towards him.

'And just how long is long-term? Do you know that you list as 'clients' corporations that have never paid you a single fee in the last ten years?'

'Do we?' Rupert was genuinely nonplussed. 'Not that I doubt your word, you understand, but…well, I suppose it's possible.'

'And that from your entertainment budget – which is over £1 million sterling a year – you devoted £600,000 to entertaining 'clients' who have paid no fees in the last five years.'

'Good God.' Rupert was genuinely shocked. He looked helplessly around the table.

'Now steady on.' It was Ben Jackson, who looked after the department's mining clients. 'Some of those clients are in cyclical industries which are suffering a downturn. In other cases we're trying to recover lost ground in the face of transaction-based marketing to our clients by the Americans. And in some cases, of course, we're entertaining non-clients, even corporates which are other firms' clients, in order to try and poach them and win business for ourselves. Those efforts can take a long time to bear fruit.'

'Gentlemen.' Fleischfresser appeared to be making a visible effort at self-control. He slurped his coffee again, but this time Rupert did not follow suit. 'Gentlemen, if you were a major corporation, and one investment bank offered to underwrite your rights issue at a twenty per cent discount to the current share price, and another offered to underwrite at a fifteen per cent discount, assuming you want the best price achievable, which would you pick?'

'The one who gave me the Wimbledon tickets!' It was Rory MacPherson, one of the livelier directors in the department. Several of the others laughed.

Fleischfresser stared at him, but did not comment and continued, 'Gentlemen, transaction-based investment banking has been the order of the day in the City of London for the past five years.' He looked around the table again, his glance lingering first on Howard, then on MacPherson. 'But the past five years seem to have passed you by.'

'That's not fair!' It was Rowntree, who was on his feet. 'This firm has a name, a reputation for integrity that cannot be bought by some team of transaction-based deal jockeys! We're part of the fabric of the City of London, and have been for nearly a hundred years. This department is widely regarded as a centre of excellence for executing complex transactions. We don't contract out the difficult stuff to law firms, the way the Americans do, we do it all in-house. If that means we have to focus on fewer transactions, so be it.

When a client hires us, he gets guaranteed quality of execution. And when a director takes on a client, he really takes them on. We don't flit about like the Americans, from deal to deal, client to client, leaving the real work in the hands of juniors. We see things through. What you have here may be old-fashioned, but it's quality, Dr Fleischfresser, quality! And I hope your colleagues in Zurich realise what it is that they've bought!'

'I agree.' It was Howard, who was also on his feet. 'We may have our little foibles, we may seem like an old-fashioned English gentlemen's club to outsiders, but the people here are of the highest quality. Our standards are second to none.'

Fleischfresser was smiling. To their surprise, he looked delighted, finally, with what he had heard.

'Good, gentlemen, good! This is what I needed to hear.' He beamed at Rupert. 'Rupert, you were…what is the expression? – ah yes, you were hiding your light! The numbers are a false friend. The truth is that this department is high quality.' He looked around at the assembled directors. 'Very high quality indeed.' Several of them nodded. 'A training in the Corporate Finance Department here carries a special seal of approval.' They were all nodding now, Rowntree and Howard most enthusiastically of all. Rupert had a peculiar feeling, almost as if he had eaten something that had disagreed with him and he knew he was going to be ill. 'In fact a training in this department would guarantee a job anywhere in the City!'

'Yes', several of them exclaimed, nodding vigorously, relieved that finally the Swiss had got it, 'yes, that's absolutely right.'

He paused, suddenly serious again, and looked slowly round the table, taking in each face in turn. Howard shifted uncomfortably. He thought to himself that Fleischfresser had a strange look in his eye *'For you, Tommy, the war is over.'*

Fleischfresser stood and turned towards Rupert.

'Rupert, gentlemen, I may as well tell you this at once. At SGB we believe in being open and clear in all matters.' He looked at Howard. 'I believe you call it 'playing a straight bat'. Suddenly the small, overweight man in the ridiculous clothes seemed menacing. 'Gentlemen, this department will be closed with immediate effect.' Around the table they gasped. 'A small skeleton staff will be required to stay on to complete existing business, where it cannot be passed on to other firms. The rest will be paid their statutory minimum redundancy payments and will be terminated immediately.' They were staring at one another, open-mouthed. 'Before finalising this decision, I wanted to meet you to see what sort of men you were, to decide for myself if I thought you had potential as business-winners in the international market place. I also needed to establish whether it would be necessary to establish special compensation arrangements for you if our decision was likely to lead to unusual hardship.' He looked at Rowntree and Howard. 'But you have persuaded me that it will not. You have convinced me that your department members are of such a high calibre that the statutory minimum is sufficient. There will be no special compensation, and of course no bonus payments.' He stood and was about to leave, when something occurred to him and he looked again at Rupert. 'Please forgive me for being so blunt and for making the announcement so openly to your directors without first consulting you.' He chuckled. 'I wanted to be sure that I would be safe in doing so. Sometimes people can be very…what shall we say?…emotional. But not these men.' He looked at Howard in his double-breasted suit and his lip seemed to curl upwards. 'These men are very civilised.'

❖ REGRETS ❖

The laughter coming from the cocktail bar had a raucous, drunken ring to it. As Lawrence entered, he had no need to look around for his team – they were the noisiest group by far, laughing and shouting, their table already crowded with half-empty wine bottles, cigar smoke swirling up towards the ceiling. Half a dozen voices called out to him.

'Hey, Tom – over here!'

'What can we get you?'

'Grab a seat, Tom!'

He smiled at their enthusiasm and their exuberance. He could have matched it himself once, but not any more. They were in their twenties, he had passed forty a few months ago. They still looked young and fit, whereas he was starting to develop a paunch and could not remember the last time he had been near a gym. They had their lives and careers ahead of them. He was jaded and cynical and was half a lifetime and a devastating divorce away from believing in the glamour and rewards of the City of London. They still looked innocent – well, relatively.

Lawrence was square-faced, with wavy hair and a broken nose that gave him a rugged, lived-in look. He was one of the firm's top mergers and acquisitions practitioners, a position that would comfortably earn him £1 million that year. But it really did not seem to matter any longer.

'Champagne!' he commanded. He picked up a wine bottle from the table and looked at it contemptuously. 'Who ordered this? We're celebrating, for God's sake. How often do we close a $10 billion acquisition?' He looked around at the grinning faces. 'Get me the wine list.'

There was an unseemly scramble and three wine lists were held out to him. He took one and flicked through it, then paused reflectively. A waiter appeared beside him.

'Now the question is, do we want to go for the Krug – they've got a nice '89 – or do we want something more delicate – there's a superb Cristal here?'

Half a dozen voices chorused back replies, but he ignored them and looked up to the waiter. 'We'll take two of each, to help us make our minds up. And bring the humidor.' He looked at some of the cigars his team were smoking. 'Some of my colleagues seem to need educating on choosing fine cigars.'

The team were half drunk already, their ties undone, their jackets kept on only in deference to the hotel rules. They were tired, but they were exuberant. Some had been up for two nights running, pulling together the final agreements – by comparison, all Lawrence had had to do was negotiate them.

He waited until the champagne had arrived and then raised his glass.

'Gentlemen,' he intoned in a voice of mock gravity, 'I would like to propose a toast.' He looked around to make sure he had their attention. 'The toast is to our beloved client, God bless him…because he's paying for this!'

They cheered and roared and clinked glasses. More champagne was ordered, more toasts drunk, the air became thick with cigar smoke. Two young women in slinky cocktail dresses came and sat at the bar and kept looking over at the group.

'Professionals,' said Lawrence contemptuously.

'So what? Doesn't it just save time, make things simpler?' It was Mark Taylor, one of the associates on the team, emboldened by drink. Lawrence looked over at the girls and shrugged to Taylor.

'Hey – I've nothing against hookers. I buy all the old arguments about them being socially useful. I'd legalise them, licence and tax them. I just wouldn't use them.'

'What's the big deal? They're all the same in the sack,

aren't they?' Others had stopped talking and were listening to the conversation now, intrigued to get Lawrence on to personal territory. 'Haven't you ever been tempted?'

Lawrence paused, his face suddenly serious.

'Yes, I was seriously tempted once.'

They crowded closer, straining to hear.

'I was in Moscow, working on the first debt-for-equity programme. It was just before my divorce.'

The more sober among them avoided his eye. This was getting into dangerous territory. Lawrence's divorce was well known in the firm. He had come home to find his wife, his college sweetheart, had been having an affair. She had confessed to him tearfully that she had become involved with a married man, it was all a terrible mistake, she had been lonely, he was always away, she was so sorry – and she had been forced to confess by the man's wife, who had discovered the affair and threatened to tell Lawrence. He had been devastated.

'I was travelling with my boss at the time, Charlie Villiers. We had a free evening and went out to see the town. There were a couple of stunning girls in a bar and they asked us if we wanted a good time. The one who attached herself to me was called Anya. She had blonde hair down to her waist, she had an engineering degree and had trained for the ballet. Her figure was to die for, she had the cutest lips, eyes to drown in and the sexiest Russian accent when she spoke English.'

He looked dazed, as if he could still see her in front of him.

'So did you?' It was a stupid question, but he was too far away to rise to it.

'No – we asked them what they'd charge us. They said $200 each. So Charlie said we'd pay them their money, but we didn't want to have sex with them. We wanted them to show us the town – all the sights we'd never see on our own.

We had just the best night ever. We had dinner in a restaurant they knew, danced in a club, listened to live jazz, went with them to a Russian gambling den. The best night ever.'

'And what happened?'

'Around 3:00 in the morning Charlie realised we'd be in big trouble the next day unless we stopped and got some rest. So we took them back to the hotel for a nightcap. They said they'd had a great time, and they wanted to give us a freebie. They said they knew some tricks that we'd never forget.'

'So what did you say?'

'We said no. Charlie said we were both married men and loved our wives very much, and thanked them for the kind offer.'

'Oh God – what a waste! So did they just go?'

'No – before they left, Anya said to me that she understood if I was faithful to my wife, and if I didn't want to go all the way, that was fine by her, but couldn't she at least give me a 'special treat' to remember Moscow by?'

'Oh no – this is too awful for words. Don't tell me you turned that down as well?'

Lawrence looked around, as if waking up from a dream, and took in the perspiring, drunken faces around him.

'Yes. I told her I loved my wife and it would be wrong.'

'Wow…'

There was a strange, almost wistful silence around the table. Taylor looked again at Lawrence.

'Tom – I know I'm half-cut, and I shouldn't say this, but that's pretty bloody impressive. How do you feel about it today when you look back on it?'

Lawrence took a long pull on his cigar. The bar was utterly silent. The waiters, the people at the other tables, the girls sitting at the bar, everyone was hanging on his next reply.

'The biggest fucking idiot on earth. My wife was off shagging a married man. Charlie fucking Villiers turned out to be fucking gay, but he only came out six months later.' He looked around the table again and said in a hoarse, half-whispered voice, '*Carpe diem*, guys – seize the day!'

⇢ MISDIAL ⇠

Nigel was just starting dessert when his mobile phone went off.

'Oh Christ,' he apologised to his pretty companion. 'Excuse me for a second, will you?'

She nodded reassuringly. Not that she had much choice – it was rare enough for a graduate trainee to be entertained to such a lavish lunch by someone so senior.

'Try the Yquem,' he suggested, nodding towards the dessert wine that the sommelier had just brought to the table. 'I won't be a moment.' He looked her up and down as he left the restaurant to receive his call. Definite potential, he thought, ripe for the plucking, as he took a final look at her long legs and long blonde hair before stepping outside.

'Andrews,' he snapped into the phone.

'Ah, Nigel, sorry to have to call you on the mobile. It's Rodney. I called your office but your secretary said you were still at lunch.'

'Rodney! How very good to hear from you. I thought you were still in Asia?' Damn that stupid temp, he swore silently to himself. She's going straight back to the agency the moment I get back.

'Not at all, old chap. I got in this morning. I'm in the car now with Sir Oliver, heading for the airport again for the board meeting in New York. I wanted to touch base to see if there's anything happening on the syndicated loan side of the house that I should know about?'

'Oh lots, Rodney, lots,' lied Nigel. 'Though I'm a bit wary about talking over a mobile, you know what these things are like. Perhaps I could call you later in New York, when we can talk on a land line.' And when I've had a chance to concoct something plausible, he thought to himself.

'Of course, old chap, of course,' Rodney chuckled. 'I

51

understand entirely. You just can't trust mobiles, can you?'

'Absolutely not, Rodney, but don't worry, I'll call you later on. I'll liaise with your office and sort out a time. I'll make sure you're fully briefed on the syndicated lending side of things before you go into the board meeting.'

'Very good, I look forward to talking to you later, old chap. Cheerio.'

Phew, thought Nigel, that was close. Now, I've got a delicious creature awaiting my attentions in the restaurant, but I really ought to get some people working on Rodney's briefing. Bugger it, they'll just have to work harder and faster when I get back. What's the point of being boss if you can't cut yourself some slack?

He sat down and smiled at his lunch guest.

'I'm so sorry.' He indicated his mobile phone, which he was putting back into his jacket pocket. 'Rodney and Sir Oliver. You know how it is.'

'Of course,' she stuttered, impressed. She blushed. She was still uncertain about the purpose of the lunch, though before the call she had been getting increasingly uncomfortable.

He leant forward across the table, raising his glass to her.

'Here's to an excellent career at Bartons,' he smiled, looking into her eyes. 'Cheers.'

'Cheers,' she replied, as they clinked glasses. Oh dear, she thought to herself, as she sipped the dessert wine, I've really had too much to drink. I do hope it isn't going to turn into what I'm thinking.

Her thoughts were interrupted once again by his mobile.

'I don't believe it!' he snapped. The mood had been shattered and other diners were looking at him with irritation. He reached inside his jacket pocket and held his mobile phone to his ear.

'Yes!!' he snapped.

At the other end he could hear two voices talking.

'Hello? Hello? Who is this?' he repeated. Still no answer, but the voices were carrying on a muffled conversation. He held the phone close to his ear and listened carefully.

She leant across the table, concerned and uncertain what to do next. The maitre d' was hovering nearby, clearly perplexed that a diner should be using a mobile phone in the restaurant.

'Who is it?' she asked.

'Shut up!' he spat. 'I think it's Rodney. He's talking to Sir Oliver.'

Nigel listened carefully, desperately trying to make out the words at the other end. Rodney must have put his mobile back in his pocket or his briefcase, and inadvertently pressed the redial button. Now Nigel had a perfect eavesdropping opportunity as the two men drove to the airport. He strained to make out the words. Rodney was talking. He could hear him saying something about syndicated loans, his name was mentioned, Sir Oliver said something...

'What is it, Nigel? Is it a message? Shall I listen? I may be able to help make it out.'

'Shut up, you silly girl! Get back to the office!'

She looked horrified and crestfallen, but he paid no attention as she ran to the cloakroom. The maître d' was still hovering nearby. Nigel looked at him with obvious annoyance and fished out his wallet. He threw a 'platinum' card on the table. 'Here, charge it!' He stood up and walked over to the restaurant door, still listening intently to the mobile.

'...and as for Nigel, I think he should definitely go on to the board in the next promotion round...he's long overdue if you ask me, possibly one of the most talented people in the firm. In the long run, I can see him running Bartons, with all that that implies...' It was clearly Sir Oliver. Nigel could hardly believe the words. '...I agree...' This was Rodney. 'He's talented, hard-working, something of a visionary from what I hear...' The next words were muffled.

Nigel listened desperately, straining to make out the words. Sir Oliver was talking again. '…yes, and eventually he'll get all that goes with it – a 'K' for starters: 'Sir Nigel' and in the end a chance at the Lords, if he plays his cards right. But that's all a long way off, of course…' The maître d' was standing by Nigel, clearing his throat loudly to get his attention, holding out the Amex slip for him to sign. Nigel scribbled his name on it and then physically put his hand on the man's shoulder to push him away.

'That's it! Outside, now, sir!' The maître d' was taller and stronger than Nigel and his voice silenced the restaurant. Nigel found himself ushered outside, where it had started to rain. He didn't care. He was straining to catch the words at the other end. If only he could record them, but his mobile had no such facility.

'…anyway, let's give him the good news on Monday, when we get back, assuming it's ratified by the board, of course…'

Suddenly the phone clicked and went dead. Nigel stared at his mobile, put it to his ear once again, listened desperately, willing it to come back to life. Had Rodney realised his mistake and hung up? Had they entered a tunnel and lost the signal? Had Rodney's mobile just 'timed out'? Nigel stared at his own mobile, then let out a great whoop of joy. He ran back into the restaurant, rushed up to the maitre d' and reached for his wallet. He pulled out £100, handed it to the man and smiled.

'I'm so terribly, terribly sorry. That was unforgivable of me.' He looked around at the other diners. 'You've got my Amex number – charge everyone's lunch to me. The whole restaurant – everyone. It's the least I can do.' He looked around. Now, where's that silly girl? Damn, she must have gone back to the office. Oh well, can't win them all. But if what I just heard is right, I'll get a second crack at her after Monday… As he walked back to the office, ignoring the pouring rain, he pondered about his home life. Perhaps this weekend he should finally take the plunge. He had a great future ahead of him, and frankly Christabel was a liability. He really didn't love her any more, despite the children. In fact he wasn't sure he was that keen on the children. Perhaps this weekend he should finally sit down and tell her…

In the car driving to the airport, Rodney was laughing. Sir Oliver was laughing too. Even their chauffeur was laughing.

'A case of '85 Krug says he's fallen for it hook, line and sinker!' Rodney turned to the chauffeur. 'Tom – you're our witness. A case of '85 Krug!'

Sir Oliver turned to Rodney. 'We'll have to talk to him together on Monday, of course, so that we can verify the outcome. I am a little concerned about how he'll take it when we fire him and say we're closing down the department.'

'Don't be concerned at all, Sir Oliver. The man's a second-rate, philandering little turd. If he was worth keeping on as head of department, he wouldn't have fallen for our little ruse, would he?'

Sir Oliver looked at Rodney. 'Let's see if he actually has fallen for it, Rodney. You could have a big surprise on Monday if he's contacted an employment lawyer and slaps a suit on you!'

Rodney chuckled. 'Not a chance. I know my man. Not a chance…'

Sir Oliver gave him a long sideways look. 'Rodney, has anyone ever told you you're a prize shit?'

Rodney chuckled. 'Once or twice, Sir Oliver, once or twice.'

✦ THE BIG BREAK ✦

The air was stale in the crowded office housing the 'pool' of graduate trainees. It was stale most days, and only got worse in the evenings. There were too many of them in there, some had to share desks, and in the evenings, when they ate pizza or Chinese while they worked, the smell of the food made the atmosphere even worse. It was not helped by the absence of windows. Their more senior colleagues joked about 'the Black Hole of Calcutta', located in the centre of the building where no natural light could penetrate. By midnight, when on a good day the luckiest of them were able to go home, they were tired, irritable and depressed. The 'glittering prizes' of a career in the City seemed far away.

Melvyn Goode was a rugby blue from Cambridge. He had rowed and boxed for his college as well as playing rugby for the University. He stood over six feet tall and cut a rugged, handsome figure. He was a few years older than most of the graduate entrants, having spent three years as a postgraduate studying for a doctorate in order to carry on rowing. The extra years and maturity gave him a critical edge over the other new entrants. He hated his work. What he enjoyed was an afternoon of rugby training with the boys, followed by a serious drinking session and then sex with one of the rugby-groupies. He looked back fondly on more happy times. His sex life had disappeared since he graduated and joined Bartons, and his rugby training had been sacrificed on the altar of the firm. He had put on nearly a stone in weight and looked pale and sickly. The only thing he had kept up was his drinking, and that had increased markedly, though only at late-night clubs which he frequented when he finally got free from work. He spent weekends in the office, trying to catch up with the incessant requests from his seniors for more analysis, more presentation books, more PowerPoint slides…

His only way of letting off steam in the office was to torment the other trainees. To his surprise, he had found that a prep-school-like atmosphere reigned in the trainee room. He was physically the biggest there, and slowly found that by throwing his weight around, he could get out of some of the more tedious and mind-numbing tasks, like running errands for the directors. The odd short, sharp, very occasionally mildly physical shock kept the recalcitrant few in line, while the weaker trainees readily accepted him as the boss. There were only three women amongst the twenty-five trainees, and all so ugly that Goode had no interest in them. In theory the trainees were supervised and assigned 'mentors' from among the more senior members of the department, but in practice no one was interested as long as the work was done and there were no complaints from the directors. The trainees rarely if ever left the office on business, and seldom received any feedback on the importance or success of the work they were doing. Overseas business trips were unheard-of, though it was widely known that many of the directors spent half their lives on aeroplanes.

'Probably collecting Airmiles,' said Goode to one of the other trainees, who dutifully laughed at the joke from 'the boss'. 'I wonder why none of us ever gets the chance to go on one of these fancy trips.'

'Probably lack of experience.' It was Ed Straker, one of the more difficult trainees, who did not always see eye to eye with Goode.

'What do you mean 'lack of experience'? Bullshit. We're all smart, or we wouldn't be here. We can hack it.' Goode was in no doubt that he could represent the bank in pretty much any situation that arose. He sighed and pushed away the presentation he was currently working on, a valuation document for the Russian natural gas supplier, KromGas.

Goode had grabbed the assignment when he had heard that Sir Oliver Barton was personally heading the team. In fact he had yet to meet Sir Oliver, and the work involved had turned out to be horrendous. The Russians were trying to float the company at a valuation that simply would not stack up against the benchmarks that international investors would apply. Repeated requests to rerun the numbers simply reconfirmed the same result. He groaned. It would be another long evening. 'You know, sometimes I wish we could each be given just one chance. One chance to really *do* something. If only we could show what we're made of. Then all this bullshit would seem worthwhile.'

His phone rang. He looked at it, irritated, and then nodded at one of the other trainees, who shrugged, picked up his own phone and tapped in the numbers to pick up Goode's line. 'I'm sorry? Say again? Yes, sir, of course, right away, sir!' He stood up, his hand shaking as he held out the phone to Goode. 'Sir Oliver Barton,' he whispered. Goode looked at him, sceptical.

'If you're bullshitting me, I'll nail you.'

He picked up his phone and, in his most composed voice, said, 'Melvyn Goode.'

'Ah, Melvyn, I'm pleased that we get to speak at last. It's Oliver Barton here. I'm calling in connection with KromGas. I've been most pleased with the work you've done. I'd like to discuss it in greater detail with you tomorrow. Are you free around 10:00?'

Goode's jaw dropped open. This *sounded* genuine. If the others were winding him up, he'd kill them. He looked around the room, searching for a clue, but found none. 'Of course, Sir Oliver, I'd be delighted.'

'Excellent. My office, ten o'clock tomorrow.' The phone clicked and went dead. Goode looked around the room.

'What was that all about?'

He smiled. 'Maybe something, maybe nothing. I think

my fairy godmother must have been listening. It might just be my ticket to Moscow.'

Goode stepped out of the lift onto the tenth floor. The carpet was deep pile, the receptionists were prettier than on his floor, and the atmosphere was discreetly hushed. He stepped forward, looking helplessly for someone to talk to.

'Excuse me, I'm Melvyn Goode. I have an appointment with Sir Oliver Barton at ten o'clock.'

'Of course, will you step this way?'

He was shown into an enormous ante-room with sofas, coffee tables and magazines.

'Do take a seat, Mister Goode. Sir Oliver will be with you shortly. Would you like a cup of coffee?'

'Er…no, thank you, I'm fine.' He looked around at the oak panelling, the paintings on the walls – could they all be originals? – and turned back to the receptionists sitting opposite the lifts. Where did they find them? Most of them were stunning, but weren't they bored working for old farts like Sir Oliver?

He heard the door open behind him.

'Ah – you must be Melvyn.'

He turned to see Sir Oliver standing in the open doorway of his office.

'Do come in. Have they offered you a cup of coffee?'

'Yes, thank you, Sir Oliver.' Goode was a full head taller than the older man, but Sir Oliver was by far the more commanding of the two. He had a disappointingly weak grip as they shook hands and sat down. Goode was nervous in case he had grasped Sir Oliver's hand too firmly – he did not want him to think he was trying to make an impact.

'Now,' Sir Oliver said, leaning forward with a friendly and engaging smile. 'Let's talk about your work.'

Goode found himself flattered by Sir Oliver's knowledge of the KromGas project, and surprised by the high regard in which he held his valuation work. He repeated his findings to Sir Oliver, emphasising that he was enthusiastic about the project, but not at all sanguine about the prospects of selling shares in KromGas to international investors.

'I see.' Sir Oliver sat back in his chair and contemplated the younger man. 'Well, you're the expert, you've done the work, and from what you've said I find it hard to disagree with your findings. The question is, how do we tell the Russians?'

Goode saw his chance and went for it. 'I could tell them, Sir Oliver! I know I'm relatively junior, but I'm the one who's been doing the groundwork. I've got the detailed knowledge of the material, and I'd be happy to walk them through it in detail. With the facts in front of them, they could hardly disagree with us, could they?'

Sir Oliver leant back and scratched his chin. 'That's an interesting suggestion. As you know, we normally prefer to field more experienced corporate financiers for such a difficult situation, but you do know the subject matter.' He got up and walked around to his desk, where he consulted a large, leather-bound diary. 'Let me see, yes, here we are. The Russians have asked for a meeting to discuss our conclusions on valuation on 17th April.' He looked at Goode. 'I must be honest with you, Melvyn, that date presents some particular difficulties for the KromGas team at Bartons. I have to be in Bermuda for the Investment Banking Divisional off-site, where I'm the keynote speaker. Rory, who's been acting as the transaction director, will be in Augusta for the Treasury Division's annual golf day. He has over a dozen clients attending. And Damien, who's been assisting Rory, will be in Bermuda with me.' He gave Goode a penetrating stare. 'At times like this, we all have to think not of ourselves, but of the firm. I think it's down to you. The question is, are you up to it?'

* * *

When he got back to the trainee room, Goode was cock-a-hoop. His first trip! Yes!!! He called over Lorna, the trainees' secretary, and informed her that he would be flying to Moscow on 16th April, staying at the Kempinski, and attending a meeting with KromGas at ten the following morning. He would need a visa, air tickets, hotel booking, currency, and of course a car to the airport. She looked at him, wondering if it was all a joke. He caught her glance and looked at her condescendingly. 'Sir Oliver Barton will sign the necessary authorisations.'

Goode stepped off the plane and searched for his name among the jostling crowd holding placards at the terminal entrance. There – 'Melvyn Goode – Bartons'. It was being held by a big man in a black leather jacket. Goode went up to him and introduced himself. 'Ah yes, this way, Mister Goode.' The man's Russian accent was so thick, so *Hollywood,* that he nearly laughed. 'VIP clearance this way, Mister Goode.' Together they went to the unmarked VIP clearance channel for which Bartons and other foreign corporations paid a premium. In no time they were through, his passport stamped, and they got into a waiting Mercedes to be driven into the centre.

'Your first time in Moscow, Mister Goode?' The Russian leant close to him, his breath smelling of onions.

'Yes, as a matter of fact, it is.'

'Excellent. My name is Georgi. I look after all Bartons people when they come to Moscow. Just tell me if there is anything you want, Mister Goode.'

Goode nodded. 'Definitely.' Then he wondered, 'In fact, I'm free this evening. I have no plans. What can a man do to enjoy himself in Moscow, when he's on his own?'

Georgi looked at him, his face a picture of seriousness.

'You like culture?'

Goode was taken aback. 'Er…of course. But as a young

man…on my own for just the one evening, what are the alternatives?'

Georgi laughed and slapped him on the back. 'Don't worry, Mister Goode. After you have checked in, I will show you Moscow.'

The girl was gyrating on his lap, grinding her naked hips into his crotch, pulling his hands to her breasts and rubbing them rhythmically against herself in time with the music.

'You like our lap dancing, Mister Goode?'

Goode, fully clothed but slightly the worse for wear, looked at Georgi's grinning face.

'I like it very much, Georgi, I like it very much.' He laughed drunkenly. 'You beat the Americans hands down. They have a 'no touching' rule in their clubs. 'Full contact' lap dancing, Moscow-style, could have won the Cold War!'

Both men laughed.

A loud buzzing was going off in his head. He rolled over and tried to bury his head under the pillow. It continued. He looked up at the clock on the bedside table. Eight o'clock. Shit. He vaguely tried to recall the previous evening. The girl! Where was the girl?! He propped himself up on one elbow and looked around the room. There was no sign of her. He tried to recall how far it had all gone. Had he done anything stupid? No, he was sure he hadn't. And anyway, he was single, he could make his own choices. His head felt fuzzy, doubtless the effect of all the alcohol, but he was used to heavy drinking and made his way to the bathroom, where he put his head under the cold water tap in the washbasin. Had they actually…? He couldn't remember. He grabbed for his wallet on the bedside cabinet. Well, he thought, as far as the guys in London are concerned, we definitely did. He looked around for his clothes. Time to get dressed. The meeting's at 10:00, Georgi's picking me up at

9:30. Time for a shower, shave, breakfast and a final read-through of the presentation.

'And so, gentlemen, you will see that the transaction as presently proposed simply does not work. The buyers will not be there. The issue will be a flop.'

He looked at the three men sitting in front of him. All three were heavily built, but dressed impeccably in tailored suits through which their massive arms and shoulders bulged. To Goode, they looked like caricatures of Hollywood heavies. One of them leant forward.

'So when do we launch the share offering? When do we have the money?'

He was nonplussed. 'Mister Markov, I don't think you understand. There won't be a share offering. There won't be any money.'

The three men looked at one another, baffled. Markov turned back to Goode. 'Mister Goode, are you crazy? Do you know who we are?'

He was unsure how to respond. His head was still throbbing, he felt hot and flustered, and he could not for the life of him see why these simple-minded Russians did not understand him. 'Mister Markov,' he began again, 'what I've said is relatively straightforward. The price you are seeking for your shares is too high. It's simply not possible to sell them for such a high price in the international markets.'

'But Sir Oliver Barton told us we could.'

Goode was momentarily taken aback. 'Well, sir, I'm sure that at the time Sir Oliver told you that, it was perfectly true. But market conditions have obviously changed considerably since you first awarded us the mandate. We have to be mindful of the market environment.'

'No! We questioned Sir Oliver very carefully on this matter. He was very clear. Bartons' price was forty per cent higher than the next highest competitor. He said his firm would deliver, or face the consequences. He said it was a matter of honour.'

'Well…sometimes things can be misunderstood in the context of a marketing presentation. We sometimes find that we pitch aggressively to win a piece of business, and subsequently have to rein in our ambitions on behalf of our clients, because the market simply doesn't match our positive spirit!'

'Are you saying Sir Oliver is a liar?'

'Certainly not!' Oh God, thought Goode, I'm in way over my depth. Beam me up, Scotty. 'If Sir Oliver says something, you can rest assured that it's true.'

'So it is you who are lying?'

'No! No – absolutely not. Neither I nor Sir Oliver would ever lie to you. We are both telling the truth. It's just that the truth changes over time. Markets change. Share prices move up and down, and investor attitudes change with them. It's simply not possible to guarantee an outcome a long time in advance.'

The three men started talking rapidly in Russian. The discussion became heated, and they kept gesturing towards him. Finally Markov reached under the table and pressed a buzzer. The door opened at the far end of the conference room and the two biggest, meanest men he had ever seen came into the room. Their wore black leather jackets and sunglasses, their necks were solid lumps of muscle, they swayed from side to side as they moved, weighed down by their huge shoulders and arms. He looked at Markov. 'Mister Markov, what's going on?'

Markov shrugged. 'Business is business. Sir Oliver will understand. He has to honour his obligations.'

The men towered over Goode. One of them seized him by the arm. He struggled but could not shift the iron grip. He stared at Markov, his voice rising with a note of panic in it. 'What's going on? What are you doing to me?'

Markov and his colleagues ignored him. They had stood and were preparing to leave.

'Wait! Wait – I can call Sir Oliver. I know where he is. Just let me make the call.'

Markov turned back towards him and glanced at his watch. 'Very well. We have a few minutes.'

The heavies released him and Goode sprang to the speakerphone on the desk. He dialled Bartons' London switchboard. 11 a.m. Moscow time, that should be 8 a.m. London time. The phone rang and rang in London. Finally someone answered in a foreign-sounding accent, 'Bartons, you're through to Security.' Goode slammed his fist on the table. 'I don't believe it! The main switchboard is always open by 8:00!' He looked at Markov, who was shaking his head. 'This is Melvyn Goode. I'm calling from Moscow. I need to speak to Sir Oliver Barton urgently.' They waited, for what seemed an age. Then they heard another ringing tone and a woman's voice answered, 'Sir Oliver Barton's office.'

'Thank God!' Goode almost sobbed into the phone. He tried desperately to recall the name of Sir Oliver's secretary – June! 'June, is that you? It's Melvyn Goode, I'm calling from Moscow! I must speak to Sir Oliver. It's a matter of life and death!'

'I'm sorry, but June's got the flu this week. My name's Alison, and I'm temping. Can I help?'

'Oh God, yes, please help! Please, please, help,' he sobbed into the telephone. 'Alison, I must speak to Sir Oliver. Put me through to his hotel in Bermuda. It's a matter of life and death and there's no time to spare.'

For a moment there was silence at the other end, and Goode imagined some dumb airhead wondering what to do. But then there was another ringing tone, and after a few rings a sleepy voice answered, 'Barton.'

'Sir Oliver!' Goode screamed into the phone. 'Sir Oliver, it's Melvyn Goode. I'm in Moscow, Sir Oliver, with

KromGas. They say they're going to do something terrible to me if we don't honour our valuation. They say it's your valuation, Sir Oliver, and they're saying I'm not honouring it. Please, please help me.' He broke into uncontrollable sobs.

'Who is this? Melvyn who? Who are you and what are you talking about? Do you know it's the middle of the night in Bermuda and you've woken me up? I have a very important game of golf in the morning and you've woken me up. Whoever you are, just do your best and think of the firm. Now leave me in peace.' The line clicked and went dead. Goode stared up into the cold, merciless eyes of Markov and his two colleagues. Markov leant forward.

'I think you should do as Sir Oliver suggests.' Goode felt an iron grip on each arm. The two heavies lifted him physically from the floor. 'Do your best and think of the firm.'

✢ SIGNING CEREMONY ✢

I hate these fucking things. Why the Japanese love their bloody formality is beyond me. Sure, they've done a big bond issue, and they've raised a lot of money – well, quite a lot, $300 million isn't bad in these markets, even if they are trading below par – but why inflict these awful bloody dinners on everyone? It's not far now to Claridge's – the cabbie's taking a short cut. I should probably tell him to slow down. Don't want to get there too early. Talking to these buggers is the most difficult part, even with a drink in my hand. And as for giving a speech – which brain scientist came up with that idea? I'm a trader, not some silky smooth corporate financier. Balls the size of melons, that's me. Give me a market and I'll trade it, and as long as I can make prices I'll make money. But this stuff is bollocks. And as for that slimeball from the Client Coverage team, wanting to 'check' my speech, I told him to go fuck himself. I'm a managing director of the firm, I run the fucking Japanese trading desk, and no slimeball from Corporate Finance checks my speeches. If his bosses all go off to Bermuda for an off-site, they'll just have to trust the rest of us to bale them out.

'Here we are, mate. That's eleven-ninety.'

'Here's twenty quid. Give us a fiver change and a receipt for twenty.'

'Thanks, mate – here you go.'

Oh well. That's probably the last decent bloke I'll see all evening. Deep breath, quick check of my notes and in we go. There they are. There's a formal receiving line. Typical. Lots of slimy bankers bowing and scraping and saying what an honour it was to be part of the deal. Christ, what some people will do to make money. Now, let's check them out. That bloke by the door, he's probably the one I'm looking for. Looks older than the rest.

'Hashimoto san?'

He covers his mouth with his hand. They do that when they

*want to laugh. Then he bows to me, but I kind of know he does-
n't mean it.*

'No, sir. I am Hashimoto san's chauffeur. Hashimoto san
is over there.'

*He points to another one standing at the end of the receiving
line. Funny little fella, short-sighted by the look of things, better
say hello.*

'Hashimoto san – welcome to London. Congratulations
on a very successful deal. I'm Dan Hooker from Bartons. I
run the Japanese trading desk.'

*Say something then, you fucker. Christ, this is hard work. I
don't think he's understood a word I've said.*

'Sir Oliver Barton personally asked me to give you his
congratulations on a great deal. He would have liked to be
here himself, but had to go to Bermuda on urgent business.'

Finally I think I'm getting through to him.

'Aaaaah, Bermuda? Sir Oriver Barton san?'

*Jesus, Mary and Joseph. I'm going to earn my money tonight.
Phew, another one's joining us, and thanks be to God this one
understands English. He's rabbiting on about Bartons' role in
the deal, how Sir Oliver is an old friend, I keep hearing the odd
name and then he turns to me to translate. Lots of head nodding,
a bow – I try to get down low, but I'm so much taller than he is –
and then we swap business cards, make a big show of reading
each other's cards, I try to look fascinated, find I'm nodding my
head too much. And then – at last – I can go on through and
grab a drink. Everyone else seems to know each other. They're all
chatting away in twos and threes around the room. Who shall I
join? I don't much fancy any of them. I end up chatting to a
waiter, nice enough bloke, Italian, he keeps topping me up with
Scotch and soda.*

'Mister Hashimoto, gentlemen, the signing ceremony
will begin shortly in the Asquith Room. Please take you
places.'

I find my name on the list and go through to sit down. This is the really boring bit. The good news is that we each get a smart Mont Blanc pen to sign with and we can keep them at the end. The lawyers pass round the documents. There are twenty of us signing altogether, one from each firm. Twenty sets of documents, two documents per set, forty signatures. Now if this was a German deal, or a French, or a Spanish, the lawyers would see to all this without us. But the fucking Japanese just love their signings. It's all an excuse to get the chairman and his wife over to London for some shopping. My hand's aching by the time we finish. I've brought my drink through and my glass is empty, but now they hand out champagne. I've done this before. We all stand and the professional smoothies from the other banks say 'Kampai!' I say 'God bless you!' and the chairman gives me a funny look. I've been here before, so I know to empty my glass quickly because before you know it we're off to the next room for supper. It doesn't do to waste fine champagne.

This next bit isn't bad. There's a good supper laid on with fine wine and we each get a present at the end. Some of these companies give away really nice things, like Walkmen or fancy china. But then I get the bad news. I check where I'm meant to be sitting and some bastard's put me next to the chairman! On my other side I've got some vice-president from Sanji Bank. Neither of them can speak English, so I sit quietly and enjoy the wine. In fact I enjoy quite a lot of it. My Italian friend keeps me topped up, so I'm doing fine by the time they serve the dessert and someone at the end of the table taps his fork on a glass. He stands up and everyone shuts up while he gives a long speech in Japanese. Fuck knows what he's saying, but they keep grunting enthusiastically, and the chairman sits with his eyes shut, nodding his head modestly. Or maybe he's just fallen asleep. Then the bloke says something else and I catch the words 'Bartons' and 'Hooker san', and they're all looking at me. Christ, I hate this stuff. I get up and fumble for my notes. I'm feeling a bit fuzzy, I wonder if I've had one too many, but my water glass is empty, so as I check out the people around the table I take a big swig of red. They all look away when I do this – God knows why, haven't they seen a man have a drink before?

'Hashimoto san, gentlemen. It's a great honour for me to be here tonight.' *I really am a bit breathless. I take another swig of red. I check my notes again.* 'In this very distinguished company. Because it is.' *I check my notes again. This is harder than I thought. I've lost my place. Bugger.* 'It's a great honour to be here tonight, and I really feel very honoured.' *The chairman's got his eyes open now. At least I've got him interested. On the other side of the table I can see some poncey smart-arse from one of the other banks whispering something to the bloke next to him. They look at me and smirk.* 'Oi – pay attention when I'm speeching…I mean talking!' *That got their attention.* 'This is a truly great company, and we are all very lucky to be here tonight.' *I look at the two smart-arses again.* 'Even you.' *They look at each other, gob-smacked. I can't help laughing. But now I'm really lost. My notes are all messed up. I had them on little cards, but now they're all out of order, and I'm definitely feeling the worse for wear. What to say? Ad lib.* 'In 1941 Japan attacked Pearl Harbor.' *Silence. Did I say that? Well, I've really got their attention now. This is tricky ground, but why not be open about it?* 'And later on, a lot of brave British lads died on the Burma railway.' *I nod at the chairman.* 'Killed by your lot. A lot of people were pretty unhappy about that.' *Quite a bit of whispering, but we all think this stuff – why not say it?* 'But then we nuked a couple of their cities.' *I'm a bit dry. Another swig of red.* 'Instant sunshine! I guess it evened up the score. Anyway, they knew they were toast if they didn't surrender, so up went the white flag! And that's all behind us now.' *There's a lot of whispering now. Fucking rude if you ask me.* 'And then, when I was still a youngster, Hiro…Hiro…Hirohito visited England. And I remember the cover of Private Eye – 'Hirohito flies in – nasty nip in the air.' 'The Eye says Piss off, bandy knees.' There just wasn't any respect.' *The chairman's whispering to the bloke on his other side. I hope he understands all this. I'm just getting to my point.* 'But you, Mister Chairman, got a very different welcome. Because times have changed. We're all friends now.' *Two of the Japanese are arguing very loudly now. One of them keeps pointing at me, shouting. The other holds him back, makes him sit down. Fucking rude. Probably can't hold his drink.* 'Now, your deal is trading below par and there are a lot of unhappy investors out there. Probably not many of these blokes here tonight have told you that. But I believe in playing a straight bat. Or maybe I should say a straight samurai sword?' *I pause for them to laugh, but no one does. They've either got no sense of humour or they can't take a joke. Or maybe both. Anyway, let's check the notes again.* 'Say something about Sir Oliver.' *They look puzzled. I'm puzzled too. I shouldn't have just read that bit out. Bugger. Time to wind up.* 'In conclusion, I'd like to propose a toast.' *I look at my glass. It's empty. My Italian friend starts to bring me a refill, but another waiter grabs his arm and pulls him back. This is awkward. What can I do?* 'May I?' *I pick up the glass of the bloke from Sanji Bank. He looks a bit surprised, but I figure it's okay. I'll get him a fresh one later.* 'Hashimoto san, gentlemen, please raise your glasses. Please join me in drinking a toast to the future success of Nippon Electric...Nippon Electric...' *Buggeration. What the fuck is this company called? Nippon Electric...Razor? Nippon Electric Toothbrush? Nippon Electric Lawnmower?*

'Nippon Electric Rail!' *I'm saved by one of the smart-arses from across the table.*

'Thank you, sir – you're a scholar! Gentlemen – Nippon Electric Rail!' *They all raise their glasses, except the bloke from Sanji Bank, because I've got his, and the Japanese look grim-faced and serious, but that's just their way. The foreign bankers are all laughing, one or two even raise their glasses to me. I knew I'd wow them. It's just practice that I need. It wasn't as bad as all that. I should do this stuff more often.*

✦ AMBITION ✦

'I think that's him now!' Paul was peering out the window, trying to see who was getting out of the limousine that had pulled into the driveway. 'Yes – it's him! Christ, darling, is everything ready?'

'Yes, yes, yes – stop panicking, Paul, and come away from there. It's not as if this is the first dinner party we've given since we got married.'

'Yes, but it is the first we've given for my new boss. He's got quite a reputation, you know. He comes across as rather camp in a sort of southern Californian way, but apparently he's a serial womaniser.' He smiled and gave her a peck on the cheek. 'So watch out!'

She smiled. 'Paul, just try to relax a little. I know there's a lot riding on this, promotion, Australia and everything, but if it all ends up in the rubbish bin, we've still got each other.' She moved to put her arms around him, but he gently pushed her away and went to answer the doorbell.

From the hall she could hear her husband talking in corporate mode, louder than normal and full of false bonhomie.

'Duane – how are you? It's so good to see you. You made it here in one piece, then – I guess deepest Clapham is off the beaten track for you.'

'Sure thing, Paul, sure thing. Nice place you have here.' The accent was soft, relaxed, the voice deep and somehow reassuring. Julia thought it almost sexy.

'Duane, do come through and meet my wife, Julia.'

A tall, handsome man entered, distinguished looking, with dark eyes, wavy brown hair and a dark moustache. He was wearing what Julia thought of as a 'Miami Vice' suit, possibly Armani, tight-fitting around the hips, broad shoulders, silky smooth. He was carrying a large bunch of lilies and what looked like a magnum of Krug.

72

'You must be Julia.' He looked her directly in the eye, piercing, penetrating, giving her the impression of authority and security. He put the bottle on the sideboard. 'Paul told me you like champagne.' He smiled. 'The flowers are for him.' He leant forward and took her hand and raised it to his lips to kiss it, never letting his eyes fall from hers.

'I'm…I'm delighted to meet you,' she said, feeling herself blushing stupidly. 'The flowers are wonderful.' She laughed. 'I'm sure Paul will like them very much.'

'Do come on through to the drawing room, Duane.' Paul ushered their guest through to what they normally called the lounge. 'Here, do take a seat. Can I get you a drink?'

Duane relaxed into an armchair. Julia found him very measured in his movements, unhurried, like a big, powerful cat. He turned towards her. 'What would Julia like?'

Paul looked up, startled. 'Oh…er, yes, of course.' He looked at Julia. 'Darling, what would you like?'

She was flustered, unsure how to take Duane's excessive courtesy. 'Well, I think Duane's wonderful champagne would be nice, don't you, darling?'

'Please don't open it on account of me,' said Duane, looking at her. 'I wanted to bring something special for the two of you. Paul is one of my key men here in London, and I just wanted the two of you to know how much I appreciate him. Keep it for a special occasion. I'd love a gin and tonic.'

'Oh,' said Julia, relieved and silently delighted that they could keep such a fine – and large – bottle for another occasion, 'I'd love to join Duane in a gin and tonic, darling.'

Paul beamed. 'Righty-ho! Two gin and tonics coming up!' He disappeared into the kitchen and they heard the ice machine clunking out ice cubes. Duane leant across to Julia, who was sitting at the other end of the sofa. 'So tell me the story of the two of you. How did you meet?' She found herself blushing again as she started to relate how Paul had been a graduate trainee, she had been temping…

It seemed no time at all before they were sitting down for supper and Julia was serving the roast. Julia was conscious that she had been doing most of the talking – encouraged by Duane – while Paul was drinking steadily. As supper progressed, conversation moved onto corporate matters.

'So Paul, how do you see things going forward? Most people say the job you took on in London was a poisoned chalice, but you grasped it and you've succeeded. But now the job's done, so what next?'

Paul nearly choked on his wine. This could not be going better. Duane not only seemed relaxed, but he was being open, expansive, even indiscreet in his observations on the other members of the management committee, which Paul had only recently joined. And he seemed to have taken a particular shine to Julia.

'Well, I really don't know.' Paul was flushed from the wine. He knew he had been drinking too much, but he had been so tense about this evening that he had drunk more than he intended. Julia kept glancing in his direction, but he ignored her. 'I need a fresh challenge. I've got a few ideas, but nothing concrete at this stage.'

Duane leant across to Julia and touched her arm. 'A man like Paul needs to be challenged. He needs constantly to be stretched, pulled in new directions.'

Julia smiled nervously and nodded. Duane had hardly touched his food, though he claimed to have enjoyed it enormously, and he had barely sipped his wine, preferring to stick to mineral water. And he kept touching her; nothing obviously untoward, of course, just small social gestures – her hand, her wrist, her elbow. On several occasions their feet had touched underneath the table, and she had found him staring at her. He had smiled and after a moment looked away to carry on listening to Paul. She could not be sure why, but she felt distinctly uncomfortable. Was he attracted to her? Did he really think she would be unfaithful to her husband? He was an attractive man, there was no doubt about that, and single, and very rich indeed, if all accounts were to be believed. But she simply could not conceive of ever being unfaithful to Paul. Poor, sweet, darling Paul. He had his faults, to be sure, but he was hers. She looked at him and smiled adoringly, hoping that Duane would take the hint.

Paul was talking again. 'So, Duane, how about coffee and a digestif in the drawing room? And are you a cigar man?'

Paul tried not to cough as Duane puffed on a large Cohiba, bought specially for the occasion as a result of an intelligence-gathering exercise before the dinner.

'Are you sure you won't have a brandy?'

'Definitely not, thank you, though you are a most generous host. But another decaff would be perfect.'

'Of course.' Paul leapt up and took Duane's cup and saucer through to the kitchen, where he needed to start another pot of decaffeinated coffee. Julia followed him.

'Darling – are you blind or something? Have you not noticed anything?'

Paul looked puzzled. 'No. Should I? What are you talking about?'

She shook her head, hardly believing what he was saying. 'Darling, have you not noticed that Duane – your boss – keeps staring at me?'

'Oh, darling, don't be ridiculous. Duane's a grown man. He's a sophisticated, senior investment banker. He would hardly go preying on his directors' wives, now, would he? Don't you think you're being ever so slightly paranoid?'

She swore under her breath. 'Paul – it's not just that he's looking at me. He's mentally undressing me! I can feel his eyes on me the whole time! And he keeps touching me, too. Any excuse and he has his hands on me! Haven't you noticed?'

'Oh, for God's sake, darling! You're definitely being paranoid. And anyway, if he really does like you, is that such a bad thing?'

She looked at him. 'Paul – just what are you saying? I may be willing to play the good corporate wife when it comes to entertaining, but that's as far as it goes!'

He rolled his eyes. 'For God's sake, you're being ridiculous. He's my boss! If he wants to ogle my beautiful wife, that's fine with me. You're mine, not his, and I'm yours.' He put his arms around her and kissed her on the nose. 'But if he wants to play footsie under the table, does it do any harm?' He shrugged. 'There's Australia to think about, after all!'

She pushed him away. 'I can't believe you just said that! For God's sake, have you taken leave of your senses? I hope it's just the drink talking!'

He stepped back, holding out his arms in a gesture of helplessness. 'What can I say? We both want the fine things in life. Where do you think the money comes from? Do you think the fairies bring it? This man pays my bonus! Sometimes we have to make sacrifices. I'm not asking you to sleep with the guy! Just be nice to him.'

He winced as she threw a half-full glass of red wine in his face. It splashed his shirt and tie.

'Oh, great! Now how do you expect me to explain this to Duane?' he asked, gesturing at the wine stain down his front.

'I really couldn't care less!' She had tears in her eyes. 'Fuck you, Paul Rogers, fuck you!'

She turned and ran from the kitchen, ignoring Duane, who sat puffing his cigar on the sofa, and disappeared upstairs. After a moment or two, Paul emerged from the kitchen, looking slightly embarrassed. He was carrying a fresh cup of coffee for Duane, and had mopped up the worst of the wine stain from his shirt.

He looked at Duane and shrugged. 'I'm sorry, she's a bit emotional. She's not usually like this. But we've had a bit of a tough time lately. The wedding was very tiring, and we're trying for a baby, you know…'

Duane sat back and smiled. He patted the sofa beside him. 'Here, come and sit down.' He took the coffee cup and put it down beside him as Paul sat down. 'Relax. These things happen. I couldn't help overhearing what you were saying in the kitchen.'

'Oh no! Oh, God, I'm sorry, Duane, so very sorry! This is so embarrassing.' For a moment Paul put his head in his hands. He looked at Duane and sighed wearily. 'I'm really, truly sorry. I so wanted tonight to be a success. I don't know what to say.'

Duane leant forward and put his hand on Paul's knee. 'Hey, Paul, who's saying the evening's been a failure? I've enjoyed it. I hope you have too. And we've gotten to know each other a little better.' He looked Paul in the eye and squeezed his knee. 'And that's what matters to me.' Paul felt a sudden, unexpected feeling of nervousness in the pit of his stomach, almost bordering on nausea. 'And there's Australia to think about, isn't there, Paul? And the money – after all, the fairies don't bring it.' Duane was leaning closer to him, their faces were only inches apart. 'You enjoy the fine things in life, don't you, Paul?' He was really close, his hand firm on Paul's knee. 'Sometimes we have to make sacrifices.' Their lips were only inches apart. 'It's not as if you have to sleep with me. Just be nice to me.'

'Oh, God,' Paul said weakly. His knees were trembling, he felt sick to his stomach, and his hands were shaking. He was drenched in perspiration. He could feel Duane's hand moving up his thigh. He closed his eyes.

'You two-faced slimeball!' Duane was on his feet, shouting. 'Do you think I have any interest in you, you piece of crap? You are one dishonest, unworthy, unrighteous son of a bitch!' Paul sat on the sofa, gasping. Duane leant forward until their faces were again only inches apart. 'Is there nothing you won't do to advance your worthless career, you scumbag?' Paul could barely breathe. He shook his head. 'N…no…' he stuttered. Duane looked down at him, a mixture of pity and disgust on his face. He looked up to see Julia standing at the foot of the stairs, her hands clasped to her face, a horrified look spoiling her beautiful features. She was looking at Paul and shaking her head, her face white with shock.

Duane walked over to the foot of the stairs. He held out his hand. 'Come with me, honey. My car's outside.'

She took his hand and walked outside with him, as if in a trance, leaving the front door open behind them. Paul heard the car engine start. He started sobbing uncontrollably and curled up into a ball on the sofa.

As the limousine pulled away, Duane looked down at the beautiful woman resting against him and then glanced back over his shoulder as the house receded into the distance. He shook his head. These Brits, he thought to himself, so transparent, so easy. Boy, was he going to have fun!

⚜ EXPENSES ⚜

'Don't look now – here he comes!'

She giggled as she leant back in her chair to allow the others to catch sight of Charles Eagleberger II, the newly appointed managing director in charge of the Healthcare team.

Lawrence sighed wearily. Dinner was going to be a bore. Sally and George, respectively the analyst and associate on the team, were lively, hard-working and bright. They were also great fun. And Stockholm was a great town. But Charles Eagleberger II had a bad reputation. Technically he was Lawrence's equal – both were managing directors – but the American's constant politicking and lobbying would probably give him an edge over Lawrence if the two fell out. Lawrence was from a different department within Corporate Finance – he was a mergers and acquisitions specialist – but that would not matter to Eagleberger, who acted as if he was next to God.

'Tom Lawrence – hey, how are you?'

The mile-wide smile and the bone-crunching handshake were transparently bogus. Eagleberger sat down at the table and spread his napkin across his lap, turning to look for the waiter.

'Charles…' Lawrence began.

'Hey, hold it, Tom – let me just get some attention over here. Europeans don't understand service. They just have no idea. We need to order dinner, run through the pitch for tomorrow's meeting, and get our heads down. Tomorrow's a big day, and we need to get it right.'

'Charles, all I wanted to do was introduce Sally Crawford and George Middleton, who are from the London office. They produced the pitch book for tomorrow and did most of the preparatory work.'

79

Eagleberger looked around, genuinely puzzled. For the first time he stared at the embarrassed pair, sitting stiffly to one side as Lawrence insisted on introducing them.

'What? Oh…hi guys.'

He turned back towards the bar and finally succeeded in attracting the waiter's attention.

'Charles,' Lawrence persisted. 'Sally is the associate on the London Healthcare team, she's been with us for just six months. George has been on board for nearly two years. I thought it would be good for them to meet you in person since you're now the global head of their sector team.'

Eagleberger turned back to the table. He still looked slightly surprised, and for the first time turned to his junior colleagues.

'Well I'm sure glad to meet you guys, but…well Tom,' he turned back to Lawrence and rubbed his chin reflectively, as if wondering how to raise an awkward subject, 'I have to be frank with you. In the States I wouldn't normally take guys like this on a pitch.'

'Oh, real'y?' Lawrence leant forward. He was a good five inches shorter than his colleague. He looked the American directly in the eye.

'Why sure. These guys are doing boot camp. They exist to write pitch books, prepare presentations, carry out research, do whatever the hell they're told. Taking them on a pitch is a waste of their time and the firm's money.'

Sally and George sat silently, trying to pretend they were somewhere else and that this was not really happening. Sally, a pretty redhead with freckles, was blushing as she stared at the tablecloth.

'Well I suppose we'll have to agree to differ, Charles. Perhaps when you see the quality of their work you'll change your mind?'

'I already did.' He reached into his briefcase and produced a copy of the pitchbook, which he tossed onto the table.

'This book's too thin. I read it on the plane over. It took me twenty minutes.'

Lawrence leant back in his chair and stared briefly at the ceiling. This was too awful for words. He looked at the American.

'Of course it's thin, Charles. That's because it's *relevant*. I asked Sally and George to cut out all the boiler-plate, all the league table nonsense from the Marketing Department, all the irrelevant credentials, and instead focus on what we really had to say to the client – the bits that are original, creative, and matter to him.'

There was a brief silence as Eagleberger stared at the Englishman.

'Well…I guess I shouldn't blame them in that case, but I have to tell you, Tom, that if we don't tell the client how good we are, you can bet none of our competitors will!'

Lawrence sighed.

'Charles,' he said, straining to remain calm and patient, 'our ideas will tell the client how good we are. Our creativity and the quality of our thinking will do that. That's how we'll win the business.'

The waiter was hovering nearby.

'We'll just have to agree to differ, Tom.' He looked almost menacingly at Lawrence. 'Let's discuss it further after tomorrow's meeting, shall we? Now – who's hungry?'

They ordered in frosty silence, Sally and George taking care not to catch either man's eye. When their food orders had been taken, the sommelier came to the table.

'Let me have that,' commanded Lawrence as he held out the wine list, uncertain who to give it to. Lawrence turned to the back of the list and scrutinised it quickly.

'A bottle of the '97 Chassagne Montrachet.' He turned to Sally and George. 'A great year, and something special for the two of you – you deserve it!'

'Now hold on.' It was Eagleberger, looking shocked again. He reached over and took the wine list. 'That's…my God, expensive! It's not as if we're entertaining clients here. We can't just fly around the world spending shareholders' money buying fine wines for employees. The firm needs to keep a tight rein on expenses. And don't forget the Healthcare team's picking up the cost of this trip. That's *my* team.' He turned to the sommelier. 'Mineral water will be fine.' He glanced at Sally and George, and added, as if by way of consolation, 'Let's have still and sparkling.'

As the sommelier turned to go, Lawrence leant forward again. 'Just a moment!' He turned back to the table. 'We'll have a bottle of the Chassagne Montrachet.' Before Eagleberger could speak, Lawrence added, 'I'll pick up the tab myself.'

By 9.30 Eagleberger headed off to bed. Lawrence looked at the other two.

'So who wants a nightcap?'

They looked at each other and shrugged. They looked flat and dejected. Sally spoke.

'Look Tom, it's really kind of you, but it really doesn't help. We have to live with this idiot – you don't.'

'And he'll take it out on us – he's a bully as well as a jerk,' added George.

Lawrence said nothing for a moment, but looked thoughtful.

'I bet he is a jerk…Okay, let's skip the nightcap. You two head off up. Don't forget we have an early start tomorrow. I'll be having breakfast in my room, but let's meet at the checkout desk at, say, six o'clock.'

George looked up. 'Isn't 6:00 a little early? Our car will be outside at 6:45.'

Lawrence stared hard at him, and for once his usual light-heartedness and humour were gone. 'Be there at 6:00 sharp.'

Lawrence was leaning on the checkout counter at five past six the next morning when Eagleberger came bounding down into the lobby. His first reaction was surprise at seeing Lawrence there before him. He was even more surprised when he saw Sally and George sitting a few yards away, glancing at the morning papers.

'Hey! Hi, guys. How are we all feeling today? Pumped up and ready to go?'

Lawrence looked at him and raised a quizzical eyebrow.

'Do you want to pay, so that we can go?'

Eagleberger looked a little unsure of himself as Lawrence signalled to the receptionist. She was a tall blonde in her early twenties, dressed in a tight-fitting black skirt, with a waistcoat and white uniform blouse that gave her an almost school-ma'm-like quality.

'Good morning, gentlemen.' She looked at Lawrence and smiled. 'I think you have already checked out, yes?'

Lawrence smiled back warmly.

'That's right. My colleague needs to check out.'

She looked at Eagleberger and smiled tightly.

'Which room were you in, sir?'

'Nine seventeen,' replied the American flatly. He leant forward on the counter and stared at the mirror behind the checkout desk with an air of affected boredom. The receptionist tapped his room number into the computer and started to read out loud.

'So, let's see. We have one overnight stay, dinner in the restaurant, breakfast this morning in your room, two international calls…' she paused and her voice hardened, '…and three videos on the pay TV.'

Lawrence turned to her, startled.

'What did you say? That last item must be a mistake.'

Eagleberger stood back from the counter, uncertain how to respond. The receptionist tapped some more numbers into the computer.

'No, sir. There is no mistake. Three movies at one hundred fifty kronor each. Do you want the titles?'

'No!' It was Eagleberger, red-faced and angry. He leant forward and hissed, 'Just print the goddamned bill!'

Lawrence turned to Sally and George.

'Okay, you two – just go and wait outside, please! This is not what you think.' He turned to Eagleberger. 'Charles – presumably there has been some mistake? I took what you said about expenses last night very seriously, and I know Sally and George did too. There must be a mistake in the hotel's billing system, surely?'

Eagleberger, perspiring and breathing hard, was at a loss for words.

'No, gentlemen, there is definitely no mistake.' It was the receptionist, her earlier friendliness replaced by an icy formality. 'I see men like this the whole time. They come here, to this hotel, they watch these filthy movies. They are sick! I don't know who is sicker, the hotel for supplying them or the men who watch them. They are disgusting.' She looked directly at Eagleberger. 'What do you do, alone in your room? Do you lie in bed and play with yourself?'

He stood paralysed, open-mouthed, bright red, searching desperately for something to say.

'Are you married? Does your wife know what you do on business trips to Stockholm?' She looked at him with open contempt. 'Well?'

Eagleberger looked first at her, then at Lawrence.

'Tom…I…'

'Don't.' Lawrence turned away, his face betraying the contempt he felt for the American. 'I had no idea…I wish I didn't know this.' He turned back to Eagleberger. 'And the worst of it, Charles, is that you're expensing it to the firm. My God, the firm shouldn't be subsidising your…habits. How many trips do you do a year, Charles?'

Before Eagleberger could answer Lawrence shook his head

and said, 'No – I don't want to know. Charles – please go and wait outside for the car with the others. I'll deal with this.'

Eagleberger, speechless, walked outside like a man in a daze. Sally and George were staring through the plate glass doors. As the doors swung shut, Lawrence turned to the receptionist.

'Perhaps it would be better if we went into the manager's office to sort this out?'

'Of course.' She was formal, correct, the earlier charm had vanished altogether.

Lawrence walked stiffly, sombrely round the counter into the office. She held the door for him and followed him into the office. He turned to her.

'YES!!!' He spun around and grabbed her and hugged her. 'You were fantastic!'

She was laughing uncontrollably, tears smudging her make-up. 'I think it worked, yes?'

'Did it work? Did it work?! Yes – I think it worked.' For a while they could hardly stand, let alone talk, so racked were they with laughter. Then Lawrence took out his handkerchief and gently wiped her eyes with it, then his own. He reached for his wallet.

'We said five thousand kronor, right? Well, here's ten – and I'll probably expense it!'

They both broke out in giggles, but she thrust the notes back to him.

'No – we said five thousand, plus dinner on your next trip.' She looked at him playfully. 'Keep the money – I've wanted to do that ever since I started in the hotel business. But I will hold you to the promise of dinner. And let's expense that!'

☆ RIFF-RAFF ☆

Oh God, he thought, at the next stop they'll probably come into first class. Already he could see that second class was full and the space between compartments was packed with people standing, talking, trying to read newspapers or science fiction paperbacks. Some were clearly builders, travelling in to work on the City's huge construction sites. Others were support staff, secretaries, settlement clerks, some of the thousands of worker bees who supported and processed the transactions that were generated by people such as him.

He was generally indifferent towards them, though some he instinctively disliked just by their appearance. A vacant-looking girl with frizzy dyed blonde hair and shocking red lipstick stood chewing gum. Probably thinking about whatever had happened in the pub last night with Wayne or Lee, or about the latest episode of some stupid soap opera. She was certainly too absorbed with her thoughts to look into first class and notice him.

A youth in a cheap, ill-fitting suit with a ridiculously narrow tie and slicked-back hair was staring at her while pretending to read some tabloid crap. Good luck to him. His idea of a good night out was probably ten pints of lager and a curry with the lads. He'd be lost at Glyndebourne or Covent Garden. What a life these people led.

As he relaxed in his seat he found himself comforted by the trappings of his position and success. He wore a dark blue chalk-stripe suit, tailored in Savile Row to flatter his widening girth. His shoes were Barkers, solid, traditional leather lace-ups, unlike the Italian slip-on brothel creepers which some of the youngsters wore. He was wearing his City Club tie, whose traditional look he preferred to the brightly coloured Hermès silk affected by his younger colleagues and by the Americans. His shirt, light blue cotton with white collar and cuffs, he had bought from Pink's in their last sale, and his Pembroke College cuff links were a cut above the fancy nonsense favoured by his flashier contemporaries. He felt comfortable, and was confident that he cut a dashing figure. He might be fifty-four years old, but he only *felt* forty-four, and that was what mattered.

They were just pulling into the next station and he could see from the crowds on the platform that first class would inevitably be invaded. He stood and took his briefcase down from the luggage rack, opened it and placed it on the empty seat next to him. Then he put his *F.T.* on the seat opposite him. There was no one else in the compartment, and he had enjoyed the peace and privacy of the journey so far. If that was all about to come to an end, then he at least wanted to maintain some distance between himself and what he jokingly referred to in his club as 'the Great Unwashed'.

He had worked for over twenty-five years in the City. It had seemed the natural thing to do once it was clear that flat feet and asthma would keep him out of the Hussars. He trained first as an accountant at what was then called Peats. After qualifying he moved to the Corporate Finance Department at Bartons, one of the great City of London merchant banks, where his uncle once ran the Treasury Department. He had been solid, rather than a star, and when others – hungrier and more ambitious than him – had been headhunted to other firms, he remained and gravitated inevitably upwards. He now ran Syndicated Loans, a specialised form of lending for large borrowers requiring more funds than one bank alone could muster. It was not the most exciting job in the City, but he had a competent team of juniors – 'my chaps' – to do the numbers for him, the hours were not unduly onerous and the margins were still sufficient to earn him a decent bonus, at least by the standards of the English merchant banks, if not the American.

It was also a very clubbable business, as banks reciprocated favour for favour in putting together their deals. This played greatly to his strengths. He was a very clubbable sort, amongst the right company, of course, and had the stamina to cope with a large lunch and an extravagant dinner on the same day – he called it 'eating for the firm', and his florid complexion and waistline were a visible testament to his efforts.

He looked up with irritation as the compartment door opened. A large builder came into the compartment, his jeans and check shirt and heavy work boots looking as out of place as his heavily stubbled head and chin. Several giggling, gum-chewing girls followed him, their accents as jarring as the smell of their bubble gum breath. One of them picked up his newspaper and without a word or a glance in his direction folded it, put it on the luggage rack and sat down opposite him. The nerve of these people! And none of them had first-class tickets! Why was there never a ticket inspector when you needed one? And then, to make matters worse, a pimply youth with a weasel face and lank, greasy hair came and stood in front of him. The scrawny specimen was wearing an embarrassingly ill-fitting brown polyester suit, his shirt collar was undone and his garishly loud orange tie was loosened. He had a rolled-up tabloid under one arm. The youth nodded at the open briefcase on the seat.

'If that's yours, move it!'

The train was moving now, it was too late to jump up and call for the guard.

He felt himself blushing. They were all staring at him. His mouth was dry. He had a peculiar feeling in the pit of his stomach.

'All right, then. *I'll* move it!'

The youth picked up his open briefcase and tipped it upside down onto the floor, scattering its contents. His favourite Mont Blanc fountain pen rolled under the seat.

One of the girls gave an embarrassed giggle. The youth grinned in her direction and made to sit down.

And suddenly someone was screaming. He realised he was standing up in the compartment and they were all looking at him, mouths open, aghast. And his knuckles hurt. He looked at his hand, and then at the bloody face of the youth lying on the floor. The youth groaned and rolled over onto his side, allowing a sticky mess of blood and saliva to roll down the side of his face.

The builder, tough and intimidating when he had entered, was holding his hands out, placating, pleading, calming.

'Easy, mate. Nothing to make a fuss about.'

And it felt good! A sudden rush of adrenalin came to him and his lips parted in a smile, though his mouth was dry. *What have I done?* He laughed. He could not understand how this had happened. He felt years younger. When had he last felt so good?

He could hear a commotion outside the compartment, and realised they had stopped at a station, though it was not a regular stop. And then, through the staring faces, two uniforms, one a railway employee, the other a policeman, sliding open the door.

'All right, sir. Things seem to have got a bit out of hand, don't they? Why don't you come with us and we'll sort everything out?'

He nearly laughed. What was this patronising garbage? Couldn't the oafish plod see what had happened?

'I really don't think that's necessary, officer. And besides, I have a meeting at 8.30 which I can't afford to miss. If you'd be kind enough to take care of this oaf, I'll leave you my card and I'm sure we can speak later.'

'I'm afraid it's not that simple, sir. You will have to come with us.'

The youth on the floor groaned and one of the girls,

emboldened by the presence of the policeman, shouted, 'He hit him! We all saw!'

Others nodded.

'Shut up, you silly girl!' he spat, staring at her venomously.

The policeman stepped forward and took him firmly by the arm.

'Come with us, please, sir.'

He was led out of the compartment, past the staring faces. What about his briefcase? His pen? His meeting? Oh God, he thought, what shall I tell the office? What shall I tell my wife? What if the papers pick this up? He felt trapped, a victim. This could not be happening to him.

And then, as the train moved off, taking the staring faces with it, he stopped on the platform and looked up at the sky. It was clear and blue and the air was fresh and today he didn't have to go to work. Suddenly he was twenty years younger. He threw his head back and laughed and laughed and laughed.

The policeman looked at him, puzzled and perhaps a little nervous.

'Don't worry, officer,' he grinned. 'I'll come quietly.'

✧ BONUS ROUND ✧

'How much?! Are you kidding, Johnson is one of our top guys! We can't give him a lousy million – he'll be out of here in a nanosecond.'

'Hey, Mark, calm down, okay? There's no need to get so worked up about these numbers. And don't personalise it so much. I know you care about the guys, but you know there's a squeeze on, the bonus pool simply isn't as big as we'd all like.'

They relaxed, though they were still looking warily at Mark.

'Okay, we'll go with the million, but don't be surprised if we have a hell of a reaction from him on bonus day – he's just bought a motherfucker of a place in the country. Someone told me it covers three English counties!'

This brought a smile and the mood seemed to lighten. There were four of them around the table: Mark Jones, the American global head of Corporate Finance, Digby Smithe, the head of Mergers and Acquisitions, Dick Greenthorne, the Canadian-born head of Client Coverage, and Paul Soames, the department's chief administrator from New York – a nobody in revenue-generating terms, but powerful because knowledge is power. They were known as the *cabalito*, and each year at this time they clustered in small glass-sided meeting rooms where the rest of the department could see them plotting, planning and running numbers.

'Digby, do your M and A guys really need to be paid so much?' Digby sat up, concerned, ready to fight to protect his troops. 'Looking at this schedule, I see two things.' Mark ran his finger down a long list of names. 'First, the average length of service in M and A is so much longer than in the department as a whole. I know we've discussed this before, but some of these guys just aren't going to leave the firm, however badly we pay them. Look at this – Euan Taylor, he's been with us fourteen years, for Christ's sake! He ain't going anywhere. Or Bill Parker, he's been here seventeen years! These guys have to get a loyalty discount.'

Greenthorne and Soames nodded their support.

'I'm sorry, Mark, but I just don't accept your argument,' countered Digby uncomfortably. 'Just because someone doesn't move firms every two years doesn't mean he has no options. It may just mean he's happy.'

'Exactly!' cried Mark triumphantly. 'And if he's happy, we don't need to stretch to keep him. So he gets a discount – Paul, I want you to run a scenario where we take the base case bonus and then deduct fifteen percent from everyone who's been here more than five years, and twenty-five percent from people who've been here ten years or more. Let's see if that gives us much spare capacity. Now, where are the problem areas?'

Paul looked down the list. 'Well, there's Tim Gregory. He nearly left for Bartons back in September. We kept him, but only after a fight.'

'I remember.' It was Dick Greenthorne, showing some real interest for the first time. 'I was involved in love-bombing him. It was a hell of a sweat to keep him. But as I recall, we didn't actually guarantee him a bonus in the end.'

'That's right,' said Paul, 'he stayed on the basis of a 'trust me' from Mark. Mark – what would you like to do?'

Mark looked at them. 'Are you guys crazy? I want to toast the bastard. No one gives us that much trouble and gets away with it. He's blown it with Bartons and no headhunter will take him seriously now. Put him down for the same number as last year, less one-third.'

Even Digby nodded his agreement to this.

'What about John Moore? He was smarter. We did have to give him a guarantee.'

'Yeah, I know.' Mark looked thoughtful. 'He's a tough bastard. What did we guarantee him?'

'One point five.'

'That much? Shit. Still, he's one mean son of a bitch. Let's put him down for one point six.'

'Is that logical?' It was Digby, reluctantly questioning Mark's decision. 'An extra hundred thousand is neither one thing nor the other.'

Mark nodded and rubbed his chin, uncertain what to do.

'One point seven five? Or keep him at one point five?' It was Paul, trying to be helpful.

Mark still looked uncertain.

'We can't take all day!' Dick was impatient to get on. 'One point seven five. He's a tough bastard, but we need tough bastards.'

'Done,' concluded Mark. 'Who's next?'

'Two of my chaps, I'm afraid,' said Digby. 'Higgins and Thorpe. They weren't promoted last year, and their bonuses really were a little light.'

'Promotion?' Mark sneered. 'Promotion? What rank are these guys?' He looked at the schedule. 'Assistant directors. Okay, make them executive directors, put up their base salaries, and raise their bonuses by ten percent.'

'Only ten percent?' Digby looked anguished.

'Sure. If these guys are concerned about promotion, let them have promotion. Most people want money, it's Brits that want gold braid. If we promote these guys, we needn't pay them. Who else?'

Paul ran his eye down the list. 'I think that's the lot. While you were talking I ran some numbers in the spreadsheet on my laptop. We're coming up about a million short on our base case.'

The four men stood and peered at the laptop. By starting with base case assumptions, looking at the numbers they felt they needed for the department, they had done a 'bottom up' bonus analysis. The figure it had produced exceeded the likely amount Mark had indicated as being available to the department by 1 million.

'Let's cut the associates' and analysts' bonuses,' suggested Dick.

Paul tapped some numbers into the laptop. 'Doesn't make much difference. If we cut them by fifty percent, it still only gives us half a million.'

'It makes a big difference to them,' protested Digby.

'Leave it out, Digby,' Mark squashed him. 'These guys are expendable. We can buy them by the yard. Do the cut, Paul.'

Paul looked at the numbers. 'We're still half a million short.'

They all looked at Mark. 'Well, we could tweak it some more, play around a bit at the edges and see what we can do, but if this is as tight as we can get it, then let's go with this. I'll take the half million off my number.'

'Very decent of you!' Digby stood and shook Mark's hand.

'Good going, buddy – thanks!' Dick slapped him on the back.

Paul said nothing.

'Okay, gentlemen, that concludes things for this year. Paul – give the numbers to Personnel. The exact timetable for bonus awards and notifications should be coming out early next week. I'll keep you posted.'

Digby and Dick stood up and left. Paul was about to leave when Mark asked him to stay behind for a moment. When the door closed, Mark turned to Paul, a big smile on his face.

'Fantastic! We did it again.' The two men, grinning, exchanged a high-five. Paul reopened the laptop and typed in a password.

'Okay, here we are, let's see,' he peered at a new column that had appeared on the spreadsheet, 'ah yes, three point five.' He looked at Mark. 'That's three point five in your departmental 'contingency fund' – happy?'

Mark grinned back. 'Very happy. If we deduct half a million for the overrun for the department, that's three million extra for the two of us. We'll do the usual seventy-thirty split. Mine will have to be agreed with the board, of course, but that isn't usually a problem. In fact last year they congratulated me and asked how I ran such a tight ship!'

Paul looked at him. 'Any special plans this year?'

'Nope.' Mark shrugged. 'I've finished the place on Long Island, but you know what they say – no matter how much you have, you can always find something to do with it!'

'Good morning. Take a seat. Now, is it Christina or Chris?'

'My friends call me Chris.'

'Fine. Well, under these circumstances I think I'll call you Christina. Now, looking at your cv I see that you went to Millfield, most impressive academic record, did a lot of skiing – must have been fun – and then came up to Cambridge to read law. And you're expecting an Upper Second in finals. So – what's gone wrong?'

'Wrong?'

'Yes. Why aren't you expecting a First?'

'Well – an Upper Second is pretty good.'

'Perhaps you don't understand. We're not looking for people who are 'pretty good' – we want our competitors to hire people who are 'pretty good'. We want the best.'

'Of course. That's why I applied to Bartons. If I'm going to be an investment banker then I want to work for the best. And I don't rule out a First by any means. I think an Upper Second is in the bag and I'm aiming to do better.'

'So presumably you'd have no objection if any eventual offer from us is conditional on you achieving a First?'

'No…of course not…though of course things can go wrong on the day. Ideally an unconditional offer would be better, but obviously it's up to you.'

'Indeed it is. Now, I see from your application form that you list numeracy among your skills. Are you numerate?'

'Definitely – I'm very comfortable with numbers.'

'What's three per cent of seventy-two?'

'Three per cent of seventy-two?'

'Yes – come on! Imagine you're having a fee discussion with a client and we're talking millions of dollars!'

'Let me think…I'm sorry, mental arithmetic was never my forte…two point…'

'Two point one six. I'll put you out of your misery.'

'I'm sorry. Why don't you try me again?'

'That's not necessary. Tell me what you do least well.'

'Least well? Oh dear…let me think about that for a moment.'

'Perhaps not for too long – this isn't mental arithmetic, and I do have to see other candidates.'

'Yes of course. Well, I suppose my biggest problem is that I try to take on too much.'

'Oh really? That seems to be a common failing. Should I take it that you can't prioritise or merely that you have no focus?'

'Well, neither really…what I meant was…'

'That you're simply over-ambitious, tenacious, don't know when to give up, aim for the highest achievements in everything you do, coming second is the same as coming last.'

'Exactly! That's exactly what I meant.'

'Yes…I thought perhaps that might be the case. Let me give you a practical problem to consider. Let's suppose you're running a trading desk at Bartons. You buy ten million shares for the firm at 100 pence a share. You go to lunch and when you come back, they've fallen to 70 pence a share. You have three choices – sell at once, taking the loss, because obviously it was a bad decision to buy them; alternatively, buy more, because if they were good value at 100 pence, they're a bargain at 70 pence; or third, sit tight, because it was your professional judgement that it was right to buy them in the first place, so you won't panic, you'll just sit it out?'

'Gosh – I've never traded before, but…well…I think if it was my professional judgement that it was right, then I'd sit it out.'

'That's the only wrong answer. A good trader should never do nothing. Buy more to average down the price of your overall holding, or just get rid of them, but never do nothing. And by the way, you'd also be fired for going off to lunch while you were running a volatile position.'

'Oh God, I'm sorry. Look – should we just end this now? I've totally messed up every question you've put to me.'

'What do you mean, 'should we just end this now?' – I thought you agreed earlier that you're tenacious? Where's your tenacity now? Do you think our business is a pushover, some children's game where you can cry for mummy if things don't go your way?'

'Oh God, this is hard.'

'Of course it's hard. What do you expect?'

'I'm sorry, darling, I just can't.'

'What do you mean, 'darling' – have you forgotten this is an interview?'

'Roger, I really can't keep this up.'

'For God's sake, darling! Just play the game, dammit!'

'Roger, I'm sorry. You know I find this hard. I'm a lawyer, not an investment banker. I know this turns you on, but it's really hard for me. Why can't we just fuck like other couples?'

'For God's sake – just play the game! I thought we'd discussed all this before! Just play along. You know how hard this was for me – I just need to face up to it, to deal with it. Help me, please. Come on, do it for me.'

'Oh God, all right, Roger. Just give me a moment.'

'That's better. Let's try again. Are you ready? Now – is it Christina or Chris?'

☀ OFF-SITE ☀

The lobby of the Sheraton Hotel in Copenhagen was crowded with investment bankers.

'What's the collective noun for investment bankers?' asked Lawrence.

'I think a baffle,' replied his colleague, Joe Smaller. 'A baffle of investment bankers!'

The two of them made their way to the registration desk to sign in and collect the conference pack and agenda. After the signing-in formalities they were directed to a large notice board where delegates had to complete a series of personal questions against their names, intended as an 'ice-breaker' by the American organisers.

'What are your two greatest achievements in life?' Lawrence paused, thinking. For a moment his eyes glazed over and he was miles away. Then he quietly wrote 'Miss A and Miss B'.

'Okay,' said his companion, 'mine'll be getting to Miss A and Miss B before Tom Lawrence.'

They laughed.

'If you were given a year's sabbatical, how would you spend it?' Lawrence again looked wistful. 'On a beach, with Miss A and Miss B.'

'Drying out!' joked his companion. 'Let's see what some of the others have written. Wow – check this out. Donaldson's written 'Winning the Excalibur takeover mandate' and 'Being named corporate financier of the year in the *Finance Mail*'. And he'd spend his year's sabbatical making his finance skills available to charities working with deprived children in the inner cities. Slimy bastard. Who's he kidding?'

They dropped off their belongings in their rooms and made their way down to the bar. Their newly appointed head of department was standing chatting to some of the younger directors, drinking a Perrier.

'Gin and tonic!' called Smaller through the crush. 'And a large one for my father,' he added, pointing to Lawrence.

'Hello, Tom. Isn't it a little early in the day for hard liquor?'

Lawrence found himself looking at his perfectly coiffed, immaculately turned out head of department, Andrew R. Scott II. He was a large, pleasant-featured man, softly spoken for an American, part of the self-styled East Coast aristocracy.

'It's never too early for a gin and tonic, Andrew – anyway, aren't we supposed to be relaxing, letting our hair down?'

'Sure, Tom, sure. Here, have you met these guys? Hey guys, let me introduce you to Tom Lawrence. Tom's one of our M and A megastars in London! Tom, let me introduce you to...'

Lawrence's eyes glazed over as he fell reluctantly into corporate mode. His companion slipped away to find a better watering hole, smirking over Scott's shoulder as he disappeared.

'...and so, to sum up, what we have to achieve over the next eighteen months is to establish a clear structure for our business, determine priority sectors and target clients, and re-align resources accordingly. Once we've achieved that, we'll be positioned to take our rightful place alongside the major Wall Street firms.'

The polite applause from the audience caused Lawrence to wake up. It had been a late night, and the first session of the day was set to be one of the most boring, so he had taken the opportunity to catnap in his seat at the back of the conference hall. Smaller nudged him. 'Watch this – get ready!'

From the podium the speaker asked, 'Are there any questions or would you prefer to wait until the end of the morning session?'

'Over here!' Smaller called out to one of the pretty usherettes carrying microphones at the side of the hall. 'Over here!' She hurried to the back of the hall and passed the microphone along the line. When it reached Smaller he passed it on further down the line. 'Stephen Donaldson!' he called, gesturing further down the line, 'Stephen Donaldson.'

Donaldson looked horrified and blushed as he was passed the microphone.

From the podium, the speaker looked out into the audience. 'I think I heard that Stephen Donaldson from our London office wants to raise a point.'

Donaldson stared at the microphone in his hand, completely at a loss for what to say.

'Stand up! Stand up!' shouted Smaller.

Donaldson dutifully complied, cleared his throat and started. 'Thank you. It was a most interesting presentation.' He looked around helplessly. 'I would just like to ask how quickly you see the reorganisation taking effect.'

'Bingo! Got him!' laughed his tormentor.

The speaker looked gravely at Donaldson. 'Stephen, I laid out the timescale at the beginning of the presentation, and I mentioned it again in my summing up. But just for the sake of clarity, let me tell you one more time, we're talking eighteen months.' The speaker looked up from the dais. 'That's eighteen months, Stephen, okay?'

A number of people laughed, chuckling at the notorious sycophant's misfortune. Donaldson muttered, 'Thank you' and sat down, looking daggers at Smaller.

Andrew R. Scott II stepped up to the podium and looked out at the audience.

'Ladies and gentlemen, for the next part of our morning session, we're going to divide into break-out groups for in-depth discussions of the topics listed in your schedules. Each group will have a facilitator and will have to appoint a spokesperson to report back to us all on the group's conclusions…'

Lawrence spent lunchtime on the phone, to Smaller's disappointment, or seeing some of the younger directors for private chats. 'You didn't miss much,' said Smaller on his return. 'They closed the bar. We had fruit juice and Perrier.'

Lawrence shrugged wearily. 'Never mind, I dare say we'll make up for it later.'

'Ladies and gentlemen,' began the conference organiser, a pretty blonde American with a syrupy accent. 'The next part of our programme is listed on your schedule as 'Team-building events'. Well, I know a number of you have been curious as to what exactly this involves.'

Smaller nudged Lawrence. 'Bonding, I hope – especially with her!'

'Well,' she continued, 'now's surprise time! We want you all to divide into groups – altogether we want six groups of twelve each. And we're all going to go on a treasure hunt. But we're not hunting for real treasure. What we're hunting is cultural treasure. The treasures of this great historic city.' Lawrence and Smaller looked at each other, raised their eyebrows and groaned. 'The purpose of this exercise is team-building, so we're introducing a competitive element. We're going to give you all lists of famous buildings, sites to visit, statues and so on, and at each of them you have to find the clue that will help you answer a question. Whichever team answers all the questions correctly gets to win a special prize.'

As the meeting broke up, Lawrence called over a number of the younger directors, mostly Mergers and Acquisitions people, from London and the other European offices. When his team were assembled, they set off. Smaller called after him. 'Hey, where are you off to? Aren't we going to be on the same team? I thought we'd just piss off round the corner and spend the afternoon drinking.'

Lawrence grinned. 'Sorry – looks like my team's full.' He looked almost sad, and Smaller, taken aback, slapped him on the shoulder. 'Hey – don't worry. I'll hook up with Grigg and Barnet – they're always good for a drink.'

The conference dinner was coming to a close. It had been a noisy affair, with a lot of alcohol consumed and much good-will exchanged between colleagues. Donaldson's group had won the team-building competition, while Lawrence's team had scored no points at all. In fact Lawrence's group had given no account of how they had spent their afternoon. Smaller and his friends were well drunk, and roared with laughter and banged on the table when Donaldson went up to collect the prize, a signed copy of *Modern Business Culture and Ethics* by C. Donald Bormann, their American Chairman. 'Ask for a loose-leaf version, so you can hang it in the gents,' cried Smaller as Donaldson self-consciously returned to his seat carrying his team's 'prize'.

Somebody banged a spoon on a glass and the noise died down. Andrew R. Scott II stood at the head of the table and tapped a microphone that had been placed in front of him.

'Is this working?'

'If you mean the conference, I'd say it's a disaster!' called Smaller, laughing uproariously at his own joke. Lawrence smiled, almost sympathetically, and leant across to him.

'Why don't you cool it for a while? Let's hear what he has to say. Take it easy, eh?'

Smaller was surprised but complied with his friend's advice.

'Ladies and gentlemen, we've come here today for the first ever global off-site of the new, integrated Corporate Finance and Investment Banking Division. We've brought together senior professionals from all over the world from parts of the organisation that previously worked entirely separately. We've heard presentations about the future, we've talked, we've thrashed out some of the big-picture issues that face us, and we've all gotten to know each other a little better.' He paused, looking down the table at Joe Smaller. 'Warts and all.'

Several people laughed and looked at Smaller, who grinned back innocently.

'What I haven't yet shared with you is my new management vision, the team of senior people whom I've selected to help me run the integrated global business. In combining the different parts of the firm that are being brought together in the current reorganisation, we're creating an enormous talent pool. But it's a pool comprised of many different cultures and backgrounds, not to mention nationalities. What we have to work towards is a single, unified culture and outlook. That doesn't mean we're in the business of creating clones. We prize individuality, providing it's expressed within a team context operating within the overall organisational structure, just as we promote our global vision within a multi-local, diverse network of offices on the ground.'

'What's he talking about?' asked Smaller, looking decidedly the worse for wear.

'Cool it, Joe,' replied Lawrence. 'Let the man have his say.'

'So who will be helping me to run this great undertaking of ours? First, and most important, my deputy, Herman Radowitz. Herman will be my deputy, based with me in New York and empowered to take decisions on my behalf in my absence. He will chair all management committees which I myself am not chairing, and will deputise for me at those committees which I normally would chair, but which I am unable to attend.'

'What?' said Smaller, confused, but Lawrence hushed him again.

'Second, Jerry Li. Jerry will run Asia-Pacific, based in Hong Kong. He will have day-to-day management authority for that region, including hiring, firing and compensation recommendations at year-end. Third, Europe. Stephen Donaldson will run Europe, based out of the London office. He will have the same authority as Jerry in Asia-Pacific.'

There was a momentary silence interrupted by a groan followed by a splashing sound as Smaller slid beneath the table and was sick. The people sitting on either side of him pushed their chairs back to avoid being splashed as he retched. 'Ladies and gentlemen,' Scott continued, grimly determined not to be put off by the interruption, 'This is my chosen team. You've heard my vision, you've heard the team I've chosen to implement that vision. If anyone around this table is less than one hundred percent enthusiastic and supportive, they should leave now!'

There was silence around the table, even from Smaller, who pulled himself up into his place and mopped his face with a napkin.

'Er-hm!' Lawrence cleared his throat. 'Should we take your words literally, Andrew?' All heads turned towards him.

'You betcha! Anyone here who is not one hundred percent behind me should leave now.' Scott was trying to sound uncharacteristically loud and aggressive, but there was a hint of uncertainty in his voice.

Lawrence looked down the table at Donaldson, who was smiling smugly, his face shining from the warmth of the dining room and too much alcohol.

'In that case, I think it's only fair that I should leave now.' Lawrence was on his feet. 'I'm sorry, but the part of the firm that I know was always a broad church, flexible, adaptable, more like a family. We had no organigrams. But we did know each other, pretty well actually, without being sent on treasure hunts together. We used to say that our only strategy was not to have a strategy. We'd look back at the deals we'd done during the year and call that our strategy. And we didn't use business school jargon all the time or hold offsites. Dinners, yes, great dinners for the whole team, but not off-sites. We kept our overheads low and our profit margins high. But I guess that doesn't matter any more.' He turned and walked slowly towards the exit.

Further down the table, with an embarrassed clearing of his throat, one of the young directors who had been on Lawrence's treasure hunt team stood up. 'I'm not going to say I'm sorry, because I don't actually think I'm going to miss any of this.' He turned to follow Lawrence. Another two stood up from Lawrence's London team, then one each from the Paris and Milan offices, then the head of M and A in Frankfurt and two of his junior directors, and finally four more from London and one from Madrid. They all followed Lawrence from the room. There was a deafening silence around the table. Scott looked deathly pale and sat down. Even Donaldson looked frightened. As the remaining directors looked up and down the table, they realised the heart of the M and A practice, the only truly profitable part of the division, had just walked out of the room. The emperor was stark naked.

A wail went up from halfway along the table. It was Smaller, and he was crying. 'Why didn't he take me?' he asked his neighbour. 'We're friends. I've known him for years. He didn't even ask me.'

Donaldson got up from his place, white-faced and shaking, and walked down the table to Smaller.

'Because he knows you for what you are, laddie, he knows you for what you are. The City's full of piss-heads. They're part of the baggage in any firm, laddie. And now he's left his baggage behind to go wherever it is he's going.' He pulled Smaller closer, ignoring the stench from his soiled jacket. 'A good man, Tom Lawrence, a superstar, some would say. I've no doubt he's taking his team somewhere or other on super-star terms with superstar packages. But he knows when to cut his losses, laddie.' Donaldson turned to look at Scott, who was sitting silent and grim-faced at the end of the table. 'Yes, he knows when to cut his losses.'

·

✧ AFTER DARK ✦

Just after 2 a.m. The house is dark. They're asleep. First I need to secure the upstairs. I walk slowly along the landing. No sounds from the bedrooms. I turn around and check again in the master bedroom. In the light cast from a street lamp outside I can make out a slumbering shape in the large double bed. Good. All clear. Now, no noise. I walk slowly and carefully back towards the top of the stairs. The key is to control your breathing. I've done this so many times that it comes easily to me now. Downstairs in the hall there's a red security light blinking on and off. The downstairs alarm's been set. I walk slowly down the stairs, taking care to stay out of range of the sensor. First priority is to sort out the alarm. No problem. The control panel is in the cupboard under the stairs. I open the cupboard door, take out a penlight and shine it on the panel. Three, six, nine, eight, four. I tap in the manufacturer's master code to disable the sensors. Wouldn't want the police coming round and spoiling things. Next, the study. The door's a bit creaky, but I take it very slowly, an inch at a time. When I'm inside, I'm equally careful about how I close it. Wouldn't do to be disturbed. The desk drawers are locked, but that doesn't bother me. It's the briefcase I'm after. It's sitting on the couch by the bookcase. A brown leather briefcase with the initials C.D.B. on it – Curry, Dylan and Butterfield, one of the country's top firms of acquisition lawyers. I try the catch. It's locked. I expected that, and it doesn't matter. It's a combination lock, and they're supposed to change the numbers regularly. But I've done my homework, and I start trying the usual possibilities – birthdays, anniversaries, home phone number. Bingo! It springs open. Inside there's a thick ring-binder of papers and an old-fashioned leather desk diary. I take out the ring-binder and shine my penlight on the cover: Project Cannonball. Where do they get these names? I flick through the documents inside. This is where my real expertise comes in. In professional circles they call me The Man With The Edge. What no one knows is where I get my edge. It's a hostile takeover, *about ten days from launch. Cannonball is a pharmaceutical company, it's in the Footsie, revenues are here, market capitalisation, balance sheet and accounts, offer timetable, everything except the name. Shouldn't take a rocket scientist to work it out, but let's see what the diary tells us. Let's see, the last few days, here we are – Wednesday 14th – Cannonball planning meeting, 11 a.m., Sir Michael Peters' office. Perfect! Sir Michael's chairman of Cordon's, the second biggest pharma company in the UK. Perfect. But who's the target? Let's see, further back, yes, here we are – Monday 5th, 10.30 a.m. Xenon Pharma briefing. They think they're so smart, these corporate lawyers. But the really smart operators are people like me. Now, I've got to make sure all these papers go back in the briefcase just the way they were. We mustn't arouse any suspicion, must we?*

What was that?! I heard something. A floorboard. There's someone outside. Christ, I'm stuck in here now. Jesus, the door's opening.

'Surprise!'

The light goes on. It's the children. They can't have been asleep after all. Standing there in their pyjamas.

'What's happening down there?'

'It's all right, it's daddy. We heard him sneaking around and we surprised him.'

She enters, still pulling on her dressing gown.

'Justin, darling, what on earth are you doing?'

She sees the ring-binder in my hand, and the open briefcase.

'Justin – what on earth – oh, my God! Those are my papers, Justin. They're confidential. Your firm isn't even involved in that deal. What on earth are you doing with them? And how did you open my briefcase?'

I search desperately for something to say, but can think of nothing. What will she do?

'Mummy, is daddy in trouble?'

She pauses and looks at me, stunned.

'Yes, darling. Very big trouble indeed.'

✧ IF YOU CAN'T TAKE A JOKE... ✧

'Hurry up, Fattie! I want my bloody coffee!'

He hobbled along as quickly as he could, but one leg seemed to refuse to bend, and his progress across the trading floor was slow and awkward. Others saw his difficulty as he squeezed down the crowded aisle, trying not to spill the tray of coffee, but no one stood aside for him. Finally he got back to the desk and started distributing the coffees to the team.

'For fuck's sake, Fattie, I said a tall, skinny latte, not a grande!'

He looked at his accuser. He seemed disappointingly unruffled.

'No – I gave you what you ordered.'

'For fuck's sake, I know what I ordered. Am I right, lads, or am I right?'

They all nodded and confirmed that he was right.

'No problem, I'll go again.' He seemed unperturbed.

'Don't bother. You fucked up once and you'll probably do it again. Just put it here and fuck off.'

He placed the coffee cup on the desk and went back to his seat at the end of the row. He found it hard to sit down because of his leg, and when he had lowered himself onto the chair one of the others called out again.

'Oi, Fattie – where's my sugar? I always have two sugars!'

'No problem. I'll get some more.'

He heaved himself up and hobbled off.

They looked at each other and laughed.

'Who is this guy, Nick? He's either Mister Unflappable or we should start calling him 'No Problem'.'

'Dunno, mate. Personnel are sitting on his papers. They say we're getting a reputation for chewing up trainees, and they reckon he might survive.'

'We've only nailed three this year, and one was a girl, so she doesn't really count.'

'Yeah, but we need to be careful. That guy Hunt had a nervous breakdown. It's good for the juniors to be kicked into shape, but we mustn't nail them all.'

As the weeks passed, they experimented with different tactics. 'Fattie', or 'Hopalong' as they sometimes called him, was sent on a variety of errands – fetching the senior traders' dry-cleaning, taking their shoes to the shoeshine man on his weekly visit to the trading floor, going on 'buttie runs' to fetch bacon rolls on mornings when they were hung over, but he seemed immune to humiliation and remained unflappable, no matter how great the provocation.

On one occasion he returned to his desk to find a screen saver installed on his computer with a graphic moving image of two men having sex. He called the IT help-desk and patiently listened as they talked him through the process of removing it. Another time his chair disappeared, then his computer, and finally his telephone. Every time he left the desk, something else was gone. He moved and sat at a vacant desk in the next aisle. One afternoon he found a Post-it note on his desk with a phone call to return, and found himself talking to a prostitute who believed he was a client, while the whole team listened in on his line. He politely declined her services.

The trickiest test was when he returned to his desk to find his e-mail open at a 'Sent' e-mail from his terminal. It was addressed to Alison Harvey, the deputy head of Compliance, and began, 'Darling squashy boobs, I want to rub my…' He closed it, called Harvey, told her it was some-one's idea of a joke and no, he had no idea who might have sent it. There was a big stink and an enquiry into that one, but everyone kept quiet. After six weeks, they were getting fed up. No one had lasted this long before, especially in the face of a concerted team effort.

'So tell us, Fattie, what did you do before Bartons?'

'I was in the army.'

'What? A fat git like you in the army? Hey lads, Fattie was a war hero! Don't tell me your gammy leg's a war wound. You're pulling my plonker, Fattie.'

He said nothing.

'Oi, Fattie – I'm talking to you. When a senior trader talks to you, you fucking answer. Now STAND UP when I talk to you!'

He dutifully struggled to his feet.

'Now fetch me a fucking coffee – and for once try to get it right. Off you go, left, right, left, right, get marching.'

They laughed as he hobbled off to fetch the coffee.

The next day they had another idea.

'Oi, Fattie – Nick wants you in his office.'

He hobbled off towards the big glass-walled corner office. Nick was waiting with two of the senior traders. The mood was sombre.

'Sit down, Fattie.'

He lowered himself carefully onto the couch. Behind him a line of faces pressed against the glass, waiting for what would happen next.

'Fattie, I've got some bad news. The boys tell me you were in the army once upon a time, and I guess that'll help with what I've got to tell you. Fattie, we're having to let you go. In fact, we're not just letting you go, Fattie, we're firing you.'

As he said this, he reached into his desk drawer and produced a revolver. He raised it towards his victim and took aim.

'Goodbye, Fattie.'

There was a 'pop' from a cap in the toy gun and they all roared. Nick was doubled up with laughter. The traders outside were in stitches.

'Oi, Fattie, what's wrong? If you can't take a joke you shouldn't have joined.'

The trainee was deathly pale, his lips were pressed tightly together and his hands were shaking. He was staring at the smoking toy gun. Then they looked down and saw the dark patch spreading across his trousers.

'Oh for fuck's sake – Fattie's pissed himself!' They were uncontrollable.

'Get up, you fat bastard.' Nick was beside himself, not sure whether to laugh or be angry. 'That's my fucking couch you're sitting on.'

He rushed forward to pull the younger man to his feet before the couch was soiled. Fattie shook himself free and hobbled from the office as fast as he could, tears in his eyes, as the traders laughed and jeered and Nick and his co-conspirators exchanged high-fives.

Fattie stayed away for the rest of the week. After two days, Nick told one of the others to call his home number, but there was no answer.

'Oh, shit – I hope he hasn't done something stupid. Nick, do you think we should go round to his place? It was a bit over the top. The poor bastard's probably too scared to show his face.'

'For fuck's sake, drop it! Like I told him, if he can't take a joke he shouldn't have joined. Let's see if he shows up on Monday.'

On Monday morning, bright and early, Fattie returned. Instead of the dress-down casual clothes they were used to seeing him in, he was wearing slacks and a dark green blazer with a badge on the pocket, and a smart striped tie. He hobbled to his position at the end of the desk. Nick looked up.

'Hey, Fattie – I'm glad you're back. We kind of missed you.'

He was pale and he looked tired, with dark shadows round his eyes.

'Are you all right?'

Still he said nothing, but looked round the team, taking in the faces.

'What's with the fancy gear, Fattie? What's the badge and tie? Not the SAS, is it?'

Nick laughed, expecting the others to join in. For once, strangely, they were silent, and everyone seemed to be staring at their screens.

'Green Jackets.'

'What? What did you say, Fattie?'

'I was in the Royal Green Jackets.'

Nick was unsure how to respond.

'Oh, all right. Well...that's fine. Nice blazer. I'm very pleased for you.'

'Until I was shot.'

'Shot?'

'Shot. In Belfast. That's why I've got so fat, you see. Can't exercise.'

'Oh...well, sure. I guess that's pretty tough.'

'Nick, I want a word. In private.'

Nick sighed.

'Oh, fuck. Don't tell me you're fucking resigning. My name'll be mud with Personnel. Let's go to my office.'

They went to the big corner office. This time there were no faces pressed against the glass. The other traders said nothing but looked at each other and raised their eyebrows.

'Take a seat, Fattie.'

'I'd rather stand. I find it easier that way.'

'Suit yourself.'

Nick relaxed in his big leather power chair.

'So what's on your mind?'

'Nick, I'm firing you.'

Nick laughed.

'Fattie, never pull the same gag twice.'

'No, you don't understand. I'm really firing you.'

Fattie reached behind his back and pulled something from

his waistband, where it had been concealed underneath his blazer. It was a revolver. Nick looked at it, stupefied.

'Fattie, I hope you're joking.' There was a note of panic in his voice. 'Fattie, if that's real, you can fucking put it down right now.'

The sound was more like an explosion than a shot. Nick was catapulted backwards out of his chair and crashed onto the carpet, arms and legs splayed. A big patch of red started to spread out from his chest as he lay face down and still.

'Fucking hell!'

It was another of the traders, standing in the doorway, staring at the body.

'I've just fired Nick.'

Fattie sounded very calm.

'I'm firing you, too.'

He fired again. Outside someone screamed. He looked from the big glass-walled office towards the desk. They were all standing, staring, open-mouthed. He raised the revolver, took careful aim, and fired again. The glass wall shattered with a great crash. He picked his way carefully over the glass and started to hobble towards the desk. There was pandemonium on the trading floor. Everyone was running to the exits, chairs were knocked over, people were screaming. And hobbling after them went Fattie, rounding them up like a half-lame sheepdog with its flock. From time to time, spotting one of his former tormentors, he fired again.

'Come on, guys!' he called, as he limped awkwardly after them, 'you know what Nick said – if you can't take a joke, you shouldn't have joined!'

⇥ THE INSIDE TRACK ⇤

A massive pair of brass balls hung above the big glass doors. They were illuminated by spotlights to make them stand out in the dark and drizzle of the early morning.

'Impressive – I hope they don't drop off and hit someone on the head!'

The driver laughed briefly at his own joke, then stopped as he caught the glance of his passenger.

'When's my regular driver back?'

'Next week, sir. He's having a week in Cornwall with the family.'

His passenger said nothing, but turned to contemplate the brasswork suspended above the entrance. The driver closed the rear passenger door and got back in to drive away, breathing a sigh of relief.

'Good morning, Mister Barnes!'

The plate glass doors swung open and a smiling uni-formed security guard stepped out to usher him inside.

'It's another filthy day, I'm afraid, sir. Still, spring isn't far away.'

Barnes said nothing, but then he never did. *Looks like he's in an even fouler mood than normal*, thought the guard, still resolutely smiling. On a good day Barnes might only shout and swear and storm around having tantrums. But on a bad day…

The lift doors opened on cue, rescuing the guard from further contact with the Prince of Darkness, as the traders called him. *Phew, that's over for another day.*

When the doors opened on the fourth floor, two smiling receptionists rushed forward to relieve him of his fine cash-mere overcoat and his scarf and gloves.

'Good morning, Mister Barnes,' they chorused.

This time he did respond.

116

'Good morning, ladies,' he growled, looking them up and down and carelessly scratching himself. 'Coffee.'

'Yes, Mister Barnes,' they chorused back, and one of them hurried off to fetch him a cup.

He walked from the reception area, through his outer office, into his inner sanctum, the room that looked into the trading floor. He had a massive antique oak desk, and behind it a leather chair that was a full six inches higher than the visitors' chairs in front of the desk – a point that mattered to a five-foot-one-inch man with a Napoleonic ego. Against one wall was a set of bookshelves full of leather-bound volumes – unread, unopened, still in the pristine condition in which they were supplied by the interior designers. On another wall were pictures of him, short, fat, balding, but uncharacteristically smiling, with various luminaries, dignitaries and other celebrities whose time and attention could be bought with the right donations. A conference table filled the far side of the room, and was dominated by an over-large bronze statue of a bull and a bear fighting – the only truly personal touch in the room. And finally there was the inevitable bank of screens showing markets, prices and news as the day unfolded around the world, as well as the firm's own trading positions and real-time profit and loss.

He slipped his jacket off, revealing bright coloured braces, put it across the back of his chair, and loosened his tie. It was a morning ritual. He barely grunted as one of the receptionists entered and put a fine bone china cup and saucer on his desk.

He looked out into the trading room. The view from his office was its most impressive aspect. The 'window' was effectively an entire wall of the office. It stretched from floor to ceiling and gave him a clear view of all the major trading desks.

The trading floor was not as large as the trading floors of

the major investment banks and stockbrokers that dominated the City of London, but it was much higher tech and the scene at 7a.m. was one of bustling, chaotic activity. Young men in shirt sleeves with their collars undone and ties hanging loosely were talking urgently into telephones, shouting across the room or running up and down the rows of dealing positions, squeezing between desks, chairs and each other in their haste. The dealing positions themselves had banks of screens in front of them, and were cluttered with telephones, microphones, keyboards and papers. There was a constant backdrop of noise coming over speakers and squawk-boxes. On the walls were giant screens and the obligatory clocks showing times around the world.

From the outer office Barnes could hear the sounds of his secretaries arriving.

'You're late!'

'I'm sorry, Mister Barnes, I missed my tube.' A stunning, Barbie doll lookalike in a Chanel suit stood in the doorway. She spoke in a coyly ingratiating way.

'Not you – get me more coffee.'

'Yes, Mister Barnes.' She disappeared.

'Mary, where are this month's P and L numbers?'

An older woman entered the room, probably in her early fifties, and sighed.

'Ronald, they're where you left them last night, on top of the Reuters screen.'

'Oh,' he looked over to the screen where the offending papers sat accusingly. 'Okay. That's all.'

She left, closing the door behind her with a determined thump to show her irritation. Mary had been with him from the beginning, and was the only employee to call him by his first name. Or to let him know when she was irritated.

He wandered over to the window to study the activity on the trading floor. This was a key part of his daily routine, and he considered it a better guide to the day's fortunes than any briefing meeting or written report. As he scanned the room he studied the individuals closely. Most did not catch his eye, though they had all noted his arrival. One or two older hands nodded in his direction. The senior traders, some of whom he had known for years, were identifiable by their sagging bellies and grey hairs. They had grown old in the markets and had lived-in, seen-it-all faces. The younger traders were mostly in their twenties, slim, hard-bodied and highly strung. Many had prematurely receding hairlines, and one or two had ponytails, though most opted for short, almost military haircuts and copied their boss's taste for red braces, Hermès ties and chunky Rolexes. There was no 'dressing down' at Barnes & Co.

There were also no women. Women were temperamental, difficult people to work with and a distraction on the trading floor. And they brought legal baggage with them. You had to be careful what you said to women. They could sue you. And so, inevitably, even the most talented women traders somehow failed the interviews for Barnes & Co.

He focused on a group of three young men on the far side of the floor. They were standing with their backs to him, and unlike just about everyone else in the room they were not shouting, waving, or otherwise animated. *Trouble,* he thought. The tallest, a fair-haired, youthful figure in a pink shirt, normally strode around the floor with athletic vigour. Now he was hunched over a computer terminal with visible sweat patches under his arms.

Barnes strode to his desk and leant across to a flying-saucer-shaped speakerphone. 'Senior traders – my office, five minutes! Jules – my office – now!'

His voice boomed across the desk-speakers on the trading floor. The young man in the pink shirt visibly jumped as he heard his name called. Julian Thomas, a twenty-six-year-old PhD in astrophysics, had never failed at anything in his life. He had the most glittering résumé with the highest scores, the top prizes and the finest references. He dated the coolest girls and went to the innermost 'in'-places. But his greatest prize, at the tender age of twenty-six, was to run Barnes & Co's junk bond portfolio.

The young man entered the office and looked guardedly at Barnes.

'Jules, you're sweating. I like a little perspiration on the trading floor, but not sweat. What's going on?'

Jules paused, flushed, swallowed hard. He thought himself tough, but he had never lost before.

'Banner Corporation's folded. Finished. Disappeared. Kaput. They're not coming back.'

Barnes looked at a screen by his desk. It was flashing black.

'Why don't I see it on the screen, Jules? Where are the numbers?'

'We…I haven't input it yet. I was checking, double-checking the terms of the bonds.'

'How many did we have?'

'Thirty million.' He paused. 'It's all gone. We'll be lucky to see 10 cents in the dollar.'

It was then that the histrionics started. *Who is he doing this for?* thought Jules as the speakerphone crashed into the bookcase. He stopped short of physical assault, but then he always did. Jules wondered what would happen if he took hold of the evil, overweight dwarf and threw him through the plate glass window onto the trading floor.

Finally a sort of calm descended on the room once again.

'Goodbye, Jules. Get the fuck out of here.'

'Goodbye, Mister Barnes. I'm sorry.'

That produced another tirade. As he left the room, Jules was treated to an explanation of how any motherfucker could be sorry, but only a real fucking trader could run a real fucking trading book and think a-fucking-head.

Barnes watched as Jules made his way back to his desk to

collect his jacket from the back of his chair and pick up a few personal belongings – a baseball cap with the logo *Barmy Barnes' Army,* which he threw into a waste-paper basket, a water pistol and a child's toy gun that had featured in some of the high-spirited horseplay that Barnes encouraged after a profitable trade. Everyone knew. As Jules left, no one caught his eye, everyone had a phone to his ear; no kind words and no high-fives.

Barnes called through to his outer office.

'Mary – get out and update the termination papers for Jules. I'm firing the motherfucker for cause!'

'They're already with Word Processing, Ronald.'

'Good.'

Sometimes he felt frustrated by Mary's anticipation of his instructions, but today he was pleased. She was very efficient, always on top of things, anticipating rather than responding. He had sometimes wondered whether to hire a younger secretary, but he knew that he could never have replaced Mary. So instead he had hired the expensive blonde in the Chanel suit. She had no real secretarial skills, but looked stunning and could just about serve a cup of coffee. He turned to see his senior traders standing uncomfortably in the doorway.

'Jules is toast. I've fired the smart-arsed motherfucker.'

No-one said anything. They shifted uncomfortably and stared at the floor, the ceiling, the smashed speakerphone, anything to avoid eye contact with the boss.

'Mike – put Ben in charge of junk bonds. Tell him to clean it up and close it down, and then fire those two motherfuckers who worked with Jules.'

One of the traders nodded.

'Sure, Mister Barnes.'

Barnes opened a large cigar case on his desk and went through the motions of lighting one, using the precious seconds to think while his traders stood in uneasy silence. It was early in the day for a cigar, but fuck it, it was not every day that he lost that much money before breakfast.

'Coffee!'

The Chanel suit appeared seconds later carrying a refill. Despite their unease, the traders followed her every movement with evident appreciation.

'So how are we going to make back what Jules has lost us?'

For a moment no one spoke, then one of the traders cleared his throat and looked at Barnes.

'Intech.'

The man who spoke was Martin Dade, who ran Barnes & Co's European Equity Trading desk. He was short, aggressive, and very determined – just the kind of trader Barnes liked.

'Do you mean the German company? The semiconductor company?'

Dade nodded.

'What the fuck do you want to do with Intech?'

'They're in a price war, boss, with their US and Asian competitors, and the market's been waiting for news on their latest high-speed chip. There should be an announcement along with the half-year results in a few days' time.'

'So?'

'So I want to fuck 'em, boss. I want to short the hell out of 'em. I want to sell those shares like they're going out of fashion – which they will be by the time I'm through. The market's spooked enough as it is, the stock's off nearly five per cent in the last week. There are rumours all over the place – just check out some of the Internet bulletin boards. I tell you, it's thin, it's fragile, I want to do a real job on 'em.'

Barnes looked at him, expressionless. He liked being called boss by the senior traders, and he liked Dade, who had great market sense and was ultra-aggressive. He wandered over to a screen and punched in some numbers.

'We've already got a small short out there. So far we're up three million. If we start selling shares we don't own in that kind of size, can we borrow enough from the big institutions to cover ourselves?'

Dade nodded confidently. 'Already taken care of, boss. I've been taking soundings already, and we can cover ourselves comfortably. Mind you, if I'm right, we'll sell massively on day one, the price will collapse, and we'll buy the shares back the same day without anyone knowing we never had them in the first place. This is a winner, boss.'

Barnes looked at Dade, grinning. 'Shall we place a big bet?'

There was silence in the room, so much so that the background noise from the trading floor seemed to fade, and the noises from the outer office seemed to disappear.

'How big is big?'

It was Ray Masterson, who ran the firm's Japanese desk. He was a consistent producer, and a great natural trader, but he did not fawn upon 'the boss' in the manner of some of the others.

'Big, Raymondo, is how big I say it is.' Barnes could see he had irritated Masterson, as he had intended to, and drew satisfaction from it.

'Right, the rest of you fuck off. Dade – stay here. Gentlemen – we've a busy day ahead of us!'

He chuckled. This would be fun. And it would also be very, very profitable. Barnes had made his name by being a maverick, a contrarian who had no respect for anyone, and the guts to take on all comers if he held a strong enough view about something. He had started in the wake of the '87 crash. At that time the firm was a start-up, a group of hungry young traders fed up with the bureaucracy and hierarchy of the established City firms. Barnes had never fitted in, but instead cruised from job to job, firm to firm, collecting like-minded misfits who had ultimately joined him in pooling their limited funds with money from some wealthy and eccentric backers to start their own firm. They opened for business in the heyday of the bull market, when it seemed impossible to lose money. Then the October crash came along and everything changed. Everyone was selling, panic reigned and people who should have known better scrambled to unload positions at almost any cost. So when he judged the time right, Barnes bought. And bought. And bought. The firm extended its credit lines, borrowed at outrageous rates, but kept buying. And at first, because they had started to buy too soon, they bled. But Barnes held firm, clinging stubbornly to his view that it was all overdone, and as the markets slowly stabilised and prices started to rise again his positions went from red to black and within days the firm was motoring. Someone was smiling on them and by Christmas they were all rich men.

The legend grew in the telling, and Barnes did his best to live the legend. He hired the brightest, sharpest people in the business. He paid them lavishly but exploited them ruthlessly. His personal life, always a low priority, was soon squeezed out altogether. He acquired all the toys: a big town house, a country estate, fast cars and a taste for rich living. The first Mrs Barnes was soon replaced with a younger, prettier and much more expensive model, though she too soon faded and after an expensive divorce he settled for a succession of glamorous 'companions'. Meanwhile the business grew as he found more and more niches to explore. He invested in technology, found friendly insurance companies to invest in the business to grow its capital base – 'my dumb friends', as he called them – and adopted an ever more aggressive stance towards the City Establishment, who envied and resented him.

Now, as he watched his senior traders going back out to the floor, he was overwhelmed with a feeling of boredom, a jaded, tired flatness that made him crave excitement.

'Okay, Dade, let's do it. But you'd better have something good up your sleeve to make this work.'

Dade smiled confidently and conspiratorially.

'Don't worry boss – I've wanted to do this for a long time. I never did like the fucking Germans.'

As he left Barnes' office, he went to the men's room, checked it was empty, and got his mobile phone from his pocket.

As trading started in the German market, it was immediately obvious that Intech was in for a tough time. As Barnes & Co started to sell in huge size and at almost any price, others followed suit, wondering what the infamous trading house knew that no one else did. Just after 10:00, an Internet bulletin board carried word that the new super-chip was a dud, and that the company would have to write off close to $1 billion. The bulletin board had no official status – it was simply an Internet site where some of the millions of individual day-traders exchanged advice and tips. One of the most regular contributors to this particular site wrote under the name Gold-miner. He had a good track record and others paid attention to his opinions. When Gold-miner suggested that Intech was in trouble and should be sold ahead of its results, several thousand individual shareholders and traders tried to sell. A similar pattern followed on several other bulletin boards. The selling pressure grew as the share price started to slide. The stock was listed and traded on the US NASDAQ exchange as well as in Frankfurt, and when the US opened and American investors started to pay attention at around lunchtime in London, the slide became an avalanche. No one wanted to own Intech. The stock fell dramatically, at times almost going into free fall when there were no buyers at all. Speculators smelt blood in the water, and by mid-afternoon the share price had fallen by almost a third. $5 billion had been wiped off the giant company's share price. At their headquarters in Frankfurt, the Intech board were said to be in a crisis meeting and were refusing to take journalists' calls.

Barnes was in his element. He was out on the trading floor, surrounded by a crowd of traders, all eyes on a screen that showed the Intech share price. He noticed that Dade kept absenting himself from the floor and on one occasion joked about all the pressure giving Dade a weak bladder. Dade laughed, but their eyes met and Barnes' mood changed. He pulled the other man aside.

'Just you be fucking careful! Don't get too fucking smart for your own good!' he hissed viciously.

In financial terms, Barnes was betting the firm. It was all going on one giant spin of the wheel. They had a huge short exposure to a single stock, and, if it all went wrong, his losses could be catastrophic. But it was not going wrong. It was going wonderfully, amazingly right. At three o'clock Barnes announced that their profit on paper was over $300 million, almost as much as they had made in the entire previous six months.

The traders cheered, recognising the moment for what it was – a historic day in the markets. After this, their reputation as a trading house would be unmatchable. They had played the market's sentiment perfectly, and had used their muscle where it counted. They were truly hammering one of Germany's biggest corporations, and they were doing it from a trading desk in London. Intech's dramatic share price crash was the lead story on all the financial news bulletins, adding to the feeding frenzy in the markets. The traders laughed and joked and told bad jokes about Germans in strange accents. Dade goose-stepped up and down the floor. The atmosphere was one of total euphoria. Already Dade had mentally bought himself a big new house and a boat. This was truly a great day.

At 3:15 one of the traders called out, 'Latest from Gold-miner – Intech's going to zero!' Even Barnes joined in the laughing and cheering.

At 3:30 Barnes looked at his watch. Intech's price was off thirty-five per cent on the day. There was only about another hour of trading left. He walked over to Dade.

'Buy!'

For a moment no one moved. All eyes were on Barnes. Then there was pandemonium. Dade and his team seized telephones and hit the buttons that would direct dial to their major counterparts in the market. All eyes were on the screen as Intech's price continued to fall. In less than ten minutes Dade had closed their position, buying back the shares they had sold short. They were home and dry. Dade was punching numbers into a calculator.

'Back of an envelope, we're up three hundred and twenty million on the day.'

Barnes pursed his lips and looked around the floor. It was a moment to savour.

'So don't stop buying now.'

Dade stopped in his tracks and the whooping and cheering of the traders subsided. For the first time Dade showed real emotion.

'Boss, we haven't had a day like this since '87.'

'I know. So let's make it an even better day, shall we?'

He turned to a short, burly-looking man in a blue and white striped power shirt and an extravagantly pink Hermès tie. Their eyes met, and Barnes nodded. Rory Chalmers, Dade's ambitious number two, pushed his former boss aside and seized a telephone to start shouting orders. Others followed his example and soon the firm was buying on a scale previously unimagined. They were the only buyer in the market, and they were taking on all comers. Barnes was trying to call the bottom of the market. He did not believe for a second that Intech's super-chip was a dud, and he knew that ultimately the market fundamentals would triumph over Dade's carefully orchestrated stampede of day-traders and short-sellers. When the market realised the extent to which Intech had been oversold, the price would bounce back. And he would clean up for a second time. He ignored Dade, who sat slumped in a corner, shaking his head and muttering silently to himself.

And still Intech's price fell.

By four o'clock their earlier profit had disappeared and they were showing a loss of over a hundred and fifty million. By 4:15 their position had almost exactly reversed itself and they were down nearly three hundred million. Intech's price had halved. The company had finally caved in and issued an announcement saying that they would be making a formal statement at five o'clock.

All eyes were on Barnes as the fateful time approached. At ten to five he lit a cigar and started pacing nervously up and down. There were big sweat patches under his arms. The mood on the trading floor was quiet and sombre. They tried to avoid catching Barnes' eye. He felt hot and loosened his tie further. He tried to think how serious this was. Their losses on paper were more than their capital base could stand. But he knew he was right. He had to be right. Intech was a real company with a real business, not one of these all-puff-and-air dotcom bullshitters. They *made* things, for fuck's sake!

'It's coming now. Here it is.'

One of the young trading assistants was looking at the screen. Barnes pushed him aside. Suddenly the screen was filled with text. Barnes stared at it.

'It's in fucking German! Who speaks fucking German?!!!' he roared.

'No, over here, boss, there's an English version coming out now.'

Barnes ran over to read it for himself. The trader who had first seen it turned away, his eyes closed.

'Oh Jesus Christ, no. No, no, no. I do not fucking believe it!'

Dade walked over to the screen.

'So that's it. The fucking stock's suspended. It *is* a dud. They're scrapping the whole super-chip programme, reporting a loss of over three billion, and they're in talks with the Japanese about being taken over.'

Barnes looked at Dade. It was over. The whole thing was over. In a few days' time, when they had to cover their borrowings and close their positions, the firm would die. Even before then, he should tell the Stock Exchange. His shoulders sagged and he seemed older, shorter and frailer than the traders had ever seen him. It had been their greatest day, but it was also their last.

'Just how much did you fucking know?'

He was angry now, and his anger centred on Dade. Dade, like the others, looked dejected, a broken man, as he stared in disbelief at the screen carrying the announcement that had ended it all. He ignored Barnes, who wandered slowly back to his office.

He closed the door and sat down. How could something that seemed so solid and unshakeable come to such a sudden end? He turned to the computer screens beside him. Price feeds from the trading floor were designed to give him an instant overview of the firm's positions. Today the screens were all red, drowned in blood from the Intech disaster. On one screen flashing stop-loss alerts blinked on and off as the computer tried to tell him to stop this madness.

'It's over.'

It was Dade, standing in the doorway, his jacket over his shoulder, his briefcase packed.

'Fuck you. You're an arsehole, Dade. And you'll be lucky not to go down for this.'

Dade sauntered into the room and sat sideways on the desk, looking down at Barnes. He turned to look out at the trading floor, which was unusually quiet as it slowly emptied.

'Boss, I won't be in trouble with anyone over this. And the reason is that I'm smart.'

'The hell you are! I know what you did when you were off the floor. You weren't taking a piss or snorting nose candy. You were making fucking calls. You didn't want to do it from the trading floor because the calls are all recorded. You think you're so fucking smart! Do you know what insider trading is? It's what you get sent to prison for, that's what! And how about market manipulation – creating false markets by spreading rumours? You set up those dumb daytraders on the Internet and you did it deliberately!'

Dade laughed, unperturbed by his boss's anger.

'Okay. So tell me this. Who do you think fucking Gold-miner is? Who do you think got those day-traders stampeding? Did you check out the other web-sites? Did you check out Bear-baiter and Bull-man? Well, guess who the registered user is behind those nicknames? It ain't fucking Martin Dade, boss. No fucking way. It's Ronald fucking Barnes, that's who it is!'

He got up and turned to leave, as Barnes stared at him, open-mouthed.

'Good luck, boss. No one deserves a break more than you.' He laughed again. 'Because when all your friends hear about this, they'll really want to rush and help you, won't they? Good luck, boss.'

'I always like a large one.'

She said the words slowly, provocatively, looking the barman up and down, her eyes lingering on his broad shoulders. He blushed. She nearly giggled, but it would have been wrong at this stage.

'One large vodka on the rocks, coming up!'

He was young, fresh-faced and cheerful, with dark curly hair, and the faintest hint of a country accent. And he had clearly never met anyone like her before. He smiled nervously and turned to attend to her drink. If she had been a cat, she would have purred. This was her sort of place. A quiet country pub, a real fire, half a dozen elderly locals and a barman with the body of a Greek god.

She saw herself as a predator. Her weeks were crazy, stress-filled and exhausting, but no one was better than her at what she did and she was well rewarded. And from time to time on 'special' weekends she dressed in her tight-fitting Gucci mini-dress, dripping with jewellery, and went on the prowl. This was her way of unwinding, far from the City. It was a very sexual thing, and she had to be in charge. The one who made the running.

The barman had been clearing away glasses from the tables outside when she had driven past. He had stopped and stared as the bright red Ferrari cruised slowly past with its personalised number plate, 2 HOT. She had turned the car around a few hundred yards up the road and returned to make a gravel-crunching entrance.

She was not conventionally pretty, as befitted a swot who had been picked on at school and bullied mercilessly. She had intense pale blue eyes and very short blonde hair, and a pale, freckled complexion. She was petite and had always felt herself to be awkward and unattractive. But while nature had been sparing with its gifts to her physically, mentally it had been extravagant in its generosity.

Clara had been the most brilliant mathematician her teachers had ever known. It had come so easily to her that she never really valued her ability. When she won a scholarship to Oxford she had begun to realise that perhaps she was onto something. And when one academic glory after another fell into her lap – prizes, a senior scholarship, ultimately the highest First for eleven years – it went some way towards compensating for all the other areas of life where she felt deficient.

Her parents were never affectionate and had not really wanted children. She was a late accident who briefly interrupted her mother's career as a barrister. At boarding school she was lonely, unhappy and always hankered after *something* that she never really identified and which was always beyond her grasp.

Lacking direction on graduation, she had drifted into investment banking almost by accident via the recruiting 'milk round' of the top universities. A big US bank had been seeking mathematicians for its London-based operation and the pay had seemed astonishingly good. On joining, she had been assigned to the swaps team, a group of highly numerate – and to some extent equally deficient – financial engineers. They ranged from her supercool, ponytailed, Armani-suited boss to a bunch of spotty geeks who sat in front of computer screens all day and got nervous, spilling coffee, whenever she went near them. She found their work almost ridiculously easy. In mathematics she had always been a lateral thinker, jumping around problems, turning them upside down and playing until the solution became obvious. Within a few months the firm's top management had recognised a special talent. In a year she was a star. Now, nearly three years on, the ponytail was gone and she ran the desk. At twenty-six she was the youngest managing director in the firm and her last bonus had taken her through the million-dollar barrier.

The ponytail had been her first lover, if that was the right term, after seizing his chance at the team Christmas party. She had found it especially pleasing to make him her first victim on taking over the team: 'Paul, I'm firing you because your dick's too small and you've no idea how to make love to a woman' – it still made her laugh. She had been briefly engaged to Jason, the head of the Convertible desk, but after three months he had tearfully confessed to being secretly gay. She was incredulous. A few months later he had left 'for personal reasons'. Rumours swept the firm, and subsequently she learnt that he had been diagnosed as HIV-positive. She was almost physically sick with fear, even after her own blood test had proved negative. Since then, she had drawn a strict line between work and play, and remained totally in control. Because she could not sustain a lasting relationship – for reasons that escaped her – her love life was best described as episodic: weekends in the country, short exotic holidays, the occasional stay-over after a business trip. But nothing permanent or even, really, satisfying – and afterwards, when it was over, she always loathed and resented the men she used.

The Greek god placed her drink on the bar in front of her. Their fingers touched briefly as she took the glass and their eyes met. She smiled as she sipped her drink.

'Perfect.'

Conversation came easily despite the obvious curiosity and sideways glances of the regulars. Three vodkas later it was almost closing time. Clara looked at her watch and gasped in mock surprise.

'Christ – look at the time! And I'm way over the limit for driving. Where the hell can I stay?'

He grinned, half-sheepish, half-knowing.

'My place is half a mile down the road. I've got a room in a cottage. I'll drive the car if you like.'

She smiled.

'Have you ever driven a Ferrari?'

He grinned back.

'No – but there's always a first time! Mind you, we'll probably wake everyone up with a motor like that.'

'So let's make an entrance!'

When she awoke she was cold and uncomfortable. The bed was too small and it was lumpy and smelly. She wondered when he had last changed the sheets or pillowcases. As a lover she rated him average. He was strong and eager, but not artful. She had been relieved when it was over and he fell asleep. The alcohol had worked its usual magic for her and she too had drifted off to sleep. Now as she fumbled for her watch she wondered what it was that had woken her. It was just after four. And then she heard it again – a cockerel crowing somewhere nearby. Damn, she thought to herself, doesn't the stupid thing know it isn't dawn yet? She found her handbag beside the bed and lit a cigarette. He turned over and started snoring softly. Damn, she thought, bloody yokel!

And as she lay there listening to him snoring, a mischievous thought sprang to mind.

She got up, dressed quickly in the semi-darkness, picked up her car keys and handbag and took out a lipstick from her bag. She wrote carefully in bright red lipstick on the mirror above the small dressing table. When she had finished, she looked at what she had written, chuckled to herself and slipped out of the door.

He stirred briefly when the powerful engine roared, but did not wake up. She drove off towards the main road, intent on finding a motel or guest house where she could shower and freshen up. As she drove along in the increasing light her mood softened and her conscience started to trouble her. She had done a silly, spiteful thing. He was not a bad man. How would he react? At lunchtime her conscience got the better of her and she called directory enquiries for the number of the pub and rang him.

It was just after 1:30, normally a quiet time on the roads, particularly on a Sunday. One of the patrolmen was eating a packet of crisps as they sat in the car, concealed in a lay-by off the dual carriageway.

'Jesus Christ!'

'What is it?' He looked up from the competition on the back of the crisp packet. 'Fucking hell!'

A red Ferrari had appeared out of nowhere. They briefly caught it on the traffic monitor, and for a fraction of a second it registered at 160 mph.

'Let's get him!'

Their engine roared as they started up and raced down the slip road onto the dual carriageway. The Ferrari was already dwindling into the distance.

'Floor it! I'll call Control – it's probably a record!'

'It's certainly a nutter, that's for sure.'

The siren was wailing as they crested a low hill and saw the Ferrari in the distance. It was coming up fast behind a big Mercedes sitting in the outside lane. The Ferrari's tail-lights came on briefly, then it flicked into the inside lane and overtook the Merc on the wrong side before accelerating away. The Mercedes slowed and pulled over to the left-hand lane as the driver spotted the flashing blue lights in his mirror and heard the wail of the siren. The Ferrari disappeared round another curve in the road.

'We've no chance. We're flat out and he's losing us. Let's see which way he goes.'

They were pushing 130 mph as they rounded the curve towards the spot where the dual carriageway divided. Even above the noise of the engine and the wail of the siren they heard a sort of metallic *crump* and saw what might have been

135

a small cloud of black smoke rising into the air. As they rounded the curve they saw the smoking remains of what had once been the Ferrari. A massive concrete pillar supported the bridge over the dual carriageway and divided the road in two. The Ferrari had ignored the road markings and gone straight into the concrete pillar at full speed. Parts of it, unrecognisable any longer as a car, were burning at the base of the pillar. Other parts were scattered over the carriageway.

'Jesus Christ!'

They slowed and stopped, blocking the carriageway, and one of them activated warning lights to stop the traffic in both directions. They summoned other units, as well as the fire brigade and, at least for the record, an ambulance. When one of them found a badly burnt number plate lying by the side of the road, he kicked it and muttered to himself, 'Too bloody hot by half.'

In the pub a crowd of young men, mostly farm labourers and gamekeepers, were standing by the bar, listening to the barman's story of his latest escapade. They were unsure whether to believe it or whether it was all another of his out- rageous made-up tales, but several of the older customers were vouching for the existence of the beautiful girl in the red sports car.

'So did you believe what she'd written? I'd have been scared shitless.'

'Nah – I didn't believe it for a second. No one who really had it would write it like that – 'Welcome to the AIDS club' – in bright red letters on the mirror. Stupid cow. When she rang me, I said no problem, told her I'd been HIV-positive for years, and I understood all about it. Told her not to worry her silly head, 'cos I never took precautions either. Even told her I liked boys and did she have a brother?'

They roared.

'What a stupid cow!'

❖ PLAYING THE GAME ❖

'Welcome to Chorley Manor! Over the next two days the managing directors of the Corporate Finance Department will be assessed in a variety of different situations. Some will be straightforward, others less so. By the time we leave here, I expect to know which of you will form part of the slimmed-down department going forward, and which of you will be asked to leave.'

The silence in the great hall was palpable. A hundred pairs of eyes stared at the imposing figure on stage, the new head of Corporate Finance, brought in by Sir Oliver Barton to introduce sweeping changes into a department that had lost its direction, not to mention its profitability.

Ryan Jones had started his career in the US Marine Corps, before going to Harvard, then on to Schleppenheimer in New York, where he eventually headed the Mergers and Acquisitions Department. He was known for his brutal management style, his ruthlessness, and the uncompromising manner in which he drove his employees. And now he had been brought in to troubleshoot an old, established British merchant bank.

Mike Pearson nudged his neighbour. 'Do you think this is a real exercise, or does he already have his list?'

His neighbour, Charles Egerton, the head of the department's Mining Industry team, shrugged.

'Beats me. I guess it gives us a chance to impress him – if we want to.'

'Of course we want to,' hissed a voice behind them.

They turned to look into the beady blue eyes of Angus MacDonald, his weasel pale face framed by his ginger curls. MacDonald was the department's arch-politician, a man who made sycophancy a high art form. There was no love lost between him and Egerton.

137

Egerton smiled and nodded at MacDonald and leant back conspiratorially to whisper something to him. MacDonald leant forward, turning his ear to catch Egerton's words.

'Go fuck yourself.'

MacDonald recoiled, his lips pressed tightly together, and glared venomously at Egerton's back as he turned back towards the podium.

Jones was speaking again.

'The first exercise which we will undertake this morning is a team-builder, intended to identify those team players best able to co-operate with one another in a competitive environment. In a moment I'll ask you to divide yourselves into teams of five. You will be given maps of the grounds of Chorley Manor. Attached to the maps you will find a list of riddles. You need to solve the riddles in order to identify locations around the grounds. There are twenty in total. At each location an empty film capsule has been hidden, and in each film capsule is a rolled-up $50 bill. The team that collects the most money wins. Gentlemen,' he paused to look at his watch, 'you will have one hour, and the clock starts ticking in five minutes.'

There was a scramble as the massed ranks of managing directors sought to divide themselves up. Within a few minutes half the department had formed themselves into teams. Some were self-selecting, based on existing team relationships or old friendships, others were more cynical, as weaker players sought to attach themselves to the sharper, more intellectual types, or to senior colleagues who were thought unlikely to be fired in any reshuffle. MacDonald quickly surrounded himself with his chosen acolytes. A few frantic individuals found themselves left out of teams, alone, and clubbed together out of necessity, one or two of them almost tearful in the face of some of their colleagues' sneers. A very small number remained seated or left to return to their rooms.

From the podium, Jones announced the time: 'Gentlemen, the clock starts ticking now. Good luck and good hunting!'

There was a crash as someone knocked over a chair in the race to leave the hall and rush for the grounds. When the final competitor had left the hall, Jones stepped down from the stage and approached a small group who had remained seated. He called over to a couple of individuals who had also stayed at the back of the hall.

They reluctantly made their way forward and sat with the others. Jones looked at them.

'Is there anyone else, who's not here, who's decided not to take part in today's events?'

Mike Pearson replied, 'Sure – Nick Moran, who covers Australia, went off to call some clients. And Richard Morse went for a kip.'

Jones nodded.

'Okay, well could I ask you to do me a favour and have them called down here to join us? And order some coffee while you're at it.'

For an instant it looked as if Pearson might simply refuse, but something about the bullet-headed Marine with his close-cropped grey hair persuaded him to get up and head off towards reception. The rest sat in uneasy silence until coffee was served and the others had joined them.

Jones stood in front of them, looking at each in turn, trying to weigh them up.

'So…gentlemen. Do I take it you disapprove of my methods, or have you just worked out you don't have a chance and given up?'

No one was in a hurry to answer. A few of them stared out of the window, not bothering to hide their boredom. One or two developed a sudden interest in their nails or their shoes, and several stared directly at Jones, not bothering to conceal their hostility.

'Have you lost your tongues?'

He was looking angry, eyeing them each in turn, as if looking for someone to attack.

'Well…' It was Nick Moran, managing to look characteristically relaxed, while at the same time conveying an air of insolence bordering on surliness. 'I guess some of us might just think that being a good investment banker doesn't necessarily involve chasing round the grounds of a stately home trying to solve riddles. Some of us might just think that executive games like that are bollocks invented by idiots who've never done a real investment banking deal in their lives.'

Jones stared directly at him.

'Most of your colleagues don't agree with you – they're out there now, endeavouring to justify their positions in this department.'

Moran snorted.

'Most of my colleagues need to – they wouldn't get a job at another investment bank in a month of Sundays.'

Jones raised a quizzical eyebrow.

'Do you always stab your colleagues in the back?'

Before Moran could answer, Mike Pearson intervened.

'No – Nick normally stabs them in the front, though only when they deserve it. If people can't take criticism, they're never going to learn anything.'

Jones was not put off.

'So does that mean that you gentlemen don't have anything to learn? Am I looking at the department's closed minds, the ones who aren't prepared to take a chance on trying something new?'

'Not at all.' It was Charles Egerton, eager to speak up alongside his friend. 'If you look around the group in front of you, we probably account for seventy per cent of the department's revenues. But we don't get paid a quarter of the department's bonus pool. Part of the crisis in this department is because Sir Oliver knows we'll almost all be out of here as soon as the bonus is paid – because we're the people who can leave. And by the way, we'll mostly take our teams with us too.'

Several of the others looked uncomfortable at Egerton's candour, but none denied what he had said. Jones sighed and sat back into a leather armchair.

'So, you gentlemen are the stars, is that right? You're so smart that you do most of the business but don't get rewarded for it. If that's really true, why haven't you left before now?'

'Loyalty.' It was Richard Morse, one of the youngest Corporate Finance directors, someone who in other circumstances might have been groomed to succeed Sir Oliver. 'It may seem odd to you, coming from Wall Street, but most of us are pretty fond of this firm. We choose to stay here, we don't have to. Most of those guys,' he gestured towards the door, through which the shouts of their colleagues could be heard coming from the grounds. 'Most of those guys don't have a choice. That's why they're running around the grounds making arses of themselves, pretending to love it.'

When Jones replied he sounded angrier, indeed almost out of control.

'BULLSHIT!' He stood and towered over Morse. 'Those guys out there are doing what they're told. I'm their boss and they're doing what I told them. You guys, you're… you're… well!' He was lost for words and threw his hands up in the air.

'We're trying.' It was Pearson. 'We don't know you, other than by reputation, but by having this conversation at all we're trying.' He leant forward, desperate to get his point across to the older man. 'We won't go running round the grounds playing executive games. We won't take part in role-playing exercises or self-analysis sessions. We won't do yoga or run over assault courses. But we will do business!

141

We know how to market to our clients, we know how to poach other firms' clients. We know how to motivate the young guys. And we care about our people and the firm, even today after all that's happened. No one here likes what's happened over the past few years. The department's accumulated too much dead wood, the market's more and more competitive and we're finding it harder to win business and to attract and keep the talent that we need. We care. But you can only bang your head against a brick wall for so long. That's what Charles was saying to you. The great thing about banging your head against a brick wall is that it's nice when you stop.'

Jones sat down again and let out a long sigh. Then he reached inside his jacket pocket and got out a list of names. It was the personnel list for the division, sorted alphabetically by rank.

'Gentlemen, kindly do me a favour and circle your names on the attached list.' He handed it to Mike Pearson.

Pearson took the list, got out a pen and looked around at the others. Jones caught the look and leant forward.

'Please don't be tempted to do anything stupid. Circle your own names, gentlemen.'

Pearson circled his name, then handed the list to Charles Egerton, who did the same. He passed the list around until they had all identified themselves.

Jones took the list, folded it and placed it back in his jacket pocket.

'Thank you. Gentlemen, I'm sure you know what this means. Your actions today, the things you've said, simply confirm my own views about this department. You leave me no choice.'

They looked around at each other glumly. They could sense what was coming.

'I have no choice at all, except to fire…' He was interrupted by the crashing of the outer door as the first teams to complete the exercise ran back into the hall, jostling with each other to be first back. They were red-faced, panting, sweating, several had mud stains on their trousers. They were all smiling, ingratiating, eager as puppies to be noticed. MacDonald pushed his way to the front, beaming and panting.

'We've finished!' he grinned, casting a malicious look at the seated group whom Jones was evidently confronting.

'As I was saying,' Jones continued, 'you gentlemen leave me no choice but to fire…' he paused and looked at the growing group of bankers crowding back into the hall, '…all of those useless, spineless, overpaid sycophants.' He stood and turned to face the returning groups.

'Gentlemen, all of you have successfully shown your mettle. Please go through to the dining hall, where Personnel are waiting to process you.' He looked at MacDonald, who was staring, speechless at what he had just heard. 'Starting with you!' He turned back to the group seated around him. 'Those guys have it easy. You gentlemen don't get off so lightly. The rest of the weekend is going to be devoted to how we turn this department around. You – ' he pointed to Pearson, ' – you will be my chief operating officer, with immediate effect. You – ' he pointed to Nick Moran, ' – you will be my head of Client Coverage, with immediate effect. And you – ' he pointed to Charles Egerton, ' – you will be head of Industry Sector Coverage, with immediate effect. Gentlemen, welcome to the brave new world. And you'd better be as good as you damned well think you are!'

She walked into his office, closing the door after her, and put his coffee on the desk in front of him. He barely acknowledged her presence, but carried on staring at the screen in front of him. Then she screamed. She screamed so loud that people heard her in all the offices nearby. He leapt to his feet, ran around the desk and held her by the shoulders.

'Good God, what's wrong? Calm down! CALM DOWN!'

She carried on screaming.

The door burst open and several people rushed in, two of them secretaries from next door, one a graduate trainee who just happened to be passing, and – worst of all – his boss, the head of the Compliance Department. Others were peering round the door, anxious to know what had happened.

'He…he…touched me,' she blubbed, tears starting to run down her cheeks.

'What?!' He stared at her, incredulous. 'What did you just say?'

'George, let me handle this.' Martin Wadham, the group head of Compliance, stepped forward and took George by the arm. 'Go and wait in my office, please, old chap.'

Wadham turned to the still-crying secretary, who was being comforted by her friends. She was a pretty black girl, probably in her mid-twenties. He had often seen her around the office, but could not recall her name.

'Why don't you take her to the sickroom? I'll get my secretary to call a doctor.'

George was crying.

'I don't believe it. I just do not believe it. She can't be saying that. It's just not true. Three years she's been working for me. Three years! I've always been fair. I may not be very communicative, but I'm a lawyer, and you know as well as I do that compliance is a pretty dry old subject.'

Wadham looked at him thoughtfully from behind his desk.

'George, we've known each other for ten years, and I believe you and trust your judgement. But George, I have to ask you one thing, and I understand if you prefer to have a solicitor present, but...well, dammit, we're friends, George, and I need to know. Did you do or say anything that might have been misconstrued?'

George looked at him, speechless. And then he broke down, sobbing and holding his head in his hands.

It was worse when he got home. He and his wife had never been as physically close as he would have liked, and that side of their relationship had died altogether once it was apparent that they could not have children. They were formal, almost distant with one another.

'George, these things don't just happen! She isn't stupid. I know that much from when I've called your office. She's sharp and she's always seemed very level-headed. What exactly did you do?'

He was speechless. He stared at her, incredulous. And then he started to cry again, and in a fit of rage he hurled his whisky glass across the room, so that it smashed against the far wall.

'That does it. George Mallows, I'm calling the police. You're unstable. I'm not staying in this house with a lunatic.'

He took another glass from the cabinet and poured himself an enormous whisky.

'Do what you want,' he said, slumping into an armchair. His expression was utterly desolate, and for a moment she almost softened, but then she looked at the smashed glass, and the whisky soaking into the carpet, and she strode from the room for the hall phone.

* * *

'Christ, George, you look a mess. Where are you staying?'

'I'm still at home, but Diane's moved out. She's gone to her sister. God, this is grim. I don't know how much longer I can take it.'

The two of them were sitting in the directors' dining room. It was unusually quiet, and none of their colleagues had joined them.

'How's Wadham been?'

'Supportive up to a point. He's taken most of my work-load off me. To be frank, I'd rather be busier. I just don't know what I'm going to do next.'

'Is she suing?'

'Yes, she's got some hotshot employment lawyer on the case – sexual harassment, sex discrimination, racial discrimination, the whole thing. She was keeping a diary, and she's handed it over to the lawyers. It's all made up, of course, but who will they believe? I just don't know any more.'

After lunch he returned to his office. Two technicians were at his desk, with Wadham. They had plugged something into the back of his computer and were busy downloading something into a laptop.

Wadham looked up almost guiltily.

'Oh, George, I'm sorry to trouble you with this, but we need to double-check one or two things. It's just a formality, of course, but we have to be certain, you understand.'

'No, I don't understand.'

He turned to one of the technicians. 'What are you doing?'

The technician looked at him curiously, unsure what to say. He looked at Wadham, who nodded.

'We're checking your Internet access. Compliance doesn't operate within the normal firewall, you have unrestricted Internet access. We're checking which sites you've visited.'

'Good God! Get out of here now, all of you. Go on, out! OUT NOW!'

They were stunned by the ferocity of his response.

Wadham stepped forward.

'Look, steady on, George, we have to do this. We don't have a choice. The bank has to protect its own position.'

'I don't care about the bank. I don't care about you. Just get the hell out of my office!'

When they had gone, he sat at his desk and stared out of the window. There was a discreet tap at the door.

'Come.'

A young man entered, probably in his early twenties, fair-haired, dressed in a suit and tie.

'Excuse me, Mister Mallows. I'm Shane Willis. I'm your temporary secretary while things are…er…up in the air.'

George's scream echoed down the hallway. He picked his computer up and threw it across the room. Then he tipped the desk over and pulled over his filing cabinet, showering papers everywhere. He picked up armfuls of files labelled 'Confidential Personnel Records – Compliance' and went to the window. He opened it, threw the files out into the air, and watched them fall the seven floors to the street below. The young man ran from the room, calling 'Mister Wadham! Mister Wadham!' as he ran.

'What can we do about George?'

Wadham sat uneasily at the big conference table in the chairman's office. Sir Oliver was fixing him with an icy stare.

'Well, sir, it's very tricky. If we go to an employment tribunal we shall almost certainly lose. The odds are always stacked against us, and in this case they'll play the race card as well as sexual harassment. Apparently she's even considering criminal charges as well.'

'Good God.' Sir Oliver got up and went to stand in front

of the giant picture window, looking out over the City.

'How long has George been with us?'

'Seventeen years. He's fifty-two. He's not a high-flyer, but he's been a good, solid performer. Until this happened, I would have said he was completely reliable.'

'Is there anything else I should know?'

'Well, there is one thing, Sir Oliver.' Wadham hesitated.

'What is it? Speak up, man!'

Wadham sighed. 'This is difficult. We got the IT department to check his Internet access. We can't say for sure that this was him, you understand – he says he leaves his terminal on all the time, even when he's not in his office – but someone has been accessing some pretty tasteless websites from his terminal.'

'Oh dear. That doesn't look very good, does it?'

'It doesn't. He denies everything, of course.'

'Well he would, wouldn't he? This is a tricky one. What's his mental state like?'

'Pretty bad. His wife's left him. I've sent him home on long-term gardening leave. He's seeing his doctor for depression. I visited him at home to see for myself, and he's in an awful state. The place is a mess, he'd been drinking heavily when I saw him. I think he's very nearly lost the plot altogether.'

Sir Oliver turned back from the window.

'All right. We'll settle. We don't need any more publicity like this. Instruct our lawyers to find out what it'll cost us. What about George?'

'Well, he's three years short of retirement. We could offer him early retirement. We could make a financial settlement, pay him out on his stock options, a generous package for loss of bonus, we could come up with something that would work.'

'Make it generous. I don't want any of this to get out.'

* * *

George stood by the front door, smiling. 'Here you are,' he said, handing the keys to the young couple. 'I hope you'll be as happy here as I was.'

They turned to see a car pulling into the drive.

'Ah, that's my lift. I must be going. Good luck, I hope you're really happy here.'

He took his suitcase and put it in the boot of the car. Then he got into the passenger seat. The driver was a young black woman.

George waved as the car pulled away, and turned to the driver.

'How are you, darling?'

He leant across and patted her stomach.

'And how's my son?'

She smiled.

'He's doing fine. And if he's as cool an operator as his mum and dad, he'll go a long way.'

⋄ WORDS ⋄

The headline in the *Evening Standard* read, 'Bartons' Fat Cats Purr.' The firm had had a monster year, and over a hundred 'top performers' had received bonuses that broke the magical million-pound barrier. On the equity trading side, the firm had for once not been 'long and wrong' – owning shares in a falling market – but on the contrary had somehow done everything right. Their profits in a constantly rising market had been so great that the firm had even tried to massage the numbers down by writing off bad debts and bringing forward expenditure on such essentials as a new corporate jet and the refurbishment of the top floor, where the chairman and the board had their offices. Just before Christmas, the senior traders had been called in to the head of the Equity division one by one to receive the sort of bonus which even they found hard to complain about.

All of which made it strange that Jack Parker, the head trader on the European desk, was sitting at his workstation crying on the first morning back after the Christmas and New Year break. Parker was an old hand on the trading floor, nearly fifty years old, greying, balding, with a beer-barrel figure and the flushed, ruddy complexion of a heavy drinker. 'Fat Jack' was well known for his alcohol capacity, and his team's Friday lunches were notorious. In the open-plan environment of the trading floor, his team exchanged embarrassed glances as they arrived and sat down to start the day's work.

'Hey, Jack – what's wrong?' It was an awkward, stilted question, from a reluctant Adam Wood, his number two.

Jack just sobbed, and put his head in his hands, burying his face from the enquiring glances.

'For fuck's sake, Jacko – come on, let's grab a coffee.'

Adam took Jack by the arm and led him off towards the coffee machine at the quieter end of the trading floor. The team watched them go, wondering if Jack had suffered some kind of breakdown, but not daring to voice their concerns out loud.

Adam led an unnaturally acquiescent Jack into a conference room at the end of the floor. He put his coffee on the table and shut the door.

'Look, mate – sit down and let's talk about it. What the fuck's wrong? Is it something at home? Is it something we can help with? You're the boss, Jack, and we'll follow you anywhere, but for fuck's sake pull yourself together and talk to me.'

Jack took a deep breath and almost visibly pulled himself together, looking up to stare mournfully at Adam, revealing his bloodshot eyes, tear-stained cheeks and the dark shadows of many sleepless nights.

'To be honest, mate, I don't know where to begin.'

Adam sighed.

'Start at the beginning, boss, okay?'

It was Jack's turn to sigh.

'June's left me.'

Adam stared at him, speechless.

'She's…what…? Why? Why would she do that to you, mate?'

June Parker had been married to Jack for nearly thirty years. They were childhood sweethearts and had grown up together in Shoreditch. She had been a beauty once, but after giving her husband four children – all now grown-up – her looks had faded and with them her liveliness and good humour. Adam had often suspected that she was the reason Jack spent so much time out drinking with the boys. His generation of trader would never touch drugs, but alcohol was different. Alcohol was where they went to bond, to support one another, and to hide. A thirty-year marriage was not something to be ended casually, quickly, or without pain. Adam looked hesitantly at his boss.

'Do you want to talk about it?'

'No, not really, mate.' Jack's voice was heavy with emotion. He almost seemed to be shaking, trembling as he spoke. 'To be honest I find the whole thing fucking embarrassing.'

'Hey, Jack – come on, you don't need to be embarrassed. We're mates, for fuck's sake. We stand by each other and help sort things out. That's what mates do. If she's left you, then she's daft. You're the two million pound man, remember? How many traders got a bonus like that?' He paused. 'Do you want to tell me why she left you?'

Jack appeared almost puzzled by the question. It was as if he was distracted, far away and dragged down by weightier matters.

'Yeah, I don't mind telling you about it.'

His eyes focused again on the here and now, as he tried to pull his thoughts together.

'You remember what happened on Christmas Eve?'

It was Adam's turn to sigh.

'Do I remember? Christ, I remember – I was wasted, utterly, totally wasted. I had the mother of all hangovers on Christmas morning.'

'Yeah, well I had worse than that. I'd told June the market was closing at midday for the Christmas holiday and I'd be home early. She'd invited the kids over and all the grandchildren were coming too. She was cooking a special dinner. I even said I'd get presents for all the grandchildren – and I did, I went to Hamleys and blew a serious wedge on all kinds of stuff the previous Tuesday.'

'I remember. So what went wrong?'

'What went wrong? You don't understand – nothing went wrong. It just didn't go quite how I'd planned it. I left on time and took the presents with me, but on the way out,

Mick van Smit and the boys from the South African desk asked me to have a quick one on the way home. One thing led to another, and I ended up catching the two minutes past midnight train, the last one home.' Jack sounded mournful and had a faraway look in his eyes, as if he was re-living the events of the fateful night. 'I was as pissed as a rat. I fell asleep on the train. Lucky for me I woke up at Audley End, saw where I was and jumped off quick. Left the bloody presents behind, though. They must have ended up at King's Lynn.'

Adam let out a long, slow breath.

'Wow, that's bad…really bad. What did June say?'

'Not much really. I was feeling like shit when I got home, and I threw up in the hall, all over the carpet. That woke her up. She came downstairs, ready to lay into me.'

'Christ, this is bad…what did you say to her?'

'Well, it's funny, really. I thought of all the things I ought to say – 'Darling, I'm really sorry, it's not my fault, it was the boys. Darling, I'll make it up to you, it'll never happen again. Darling, this is the last time, from now on I'm on the wagon.' You know the sort of stuff.'

'Sure…sure.'

'But instead I looked at her and I thought about how she nagged me from morning till night, always bloody com-plaining, just a fat sullen cow, not the girl I married all those years ago, and…well…the words just came out.'

'What words?'

'I looked at her real hard and I said, 'Why don't you fuck-ing shut up?' Then I went upstairs, into the bedroom, closed the bedroom door and locked it, and slept like a log. Woke up about 10:00 the next day and she was gone. Left me a note, but that's about it.'

'Christ, mate. Christmas must have been terrible.'

'What?' Jack was looking at Adam, totally baffled by his response. 'What do you mean?'

'Well, mate…what with it being Christmas, and June walking out like that – it must have been terrible.'

Jack stared at him and shook his head slowly, as if marvelling at his stupidity.

'No, mate. No, it was not terrible. It was fucking ace! It was so fucking brilliant, I nearly killed myself. I spent Christmas Day sleeping it off, then I booked a first-class ticket to Bangkok, a suite at the Mandarin, and spent the next ten days shagging my bollocks off. It was great. I'm a free man!'

Adam stared at him, baffled, fearing for his sanity.

'Adam, you don't get it, do you? I was married to that bitch for thirty years. I'll be fifty this year. Look at me – I'm a fat old bastard. I look and I feel years older than I should. My brother's four years older than me, and he looks ten years younger. And you know why? Because he never got fucking married, that's why! Sure, June was great once upon a time, and I love the kids, but look at June now. She's a nagging, bitching, moaning cow. She doesn't really love me any more, and I don't love her. But I've got a £2 million bonus that she doesn't know about, and now I'm free. I'm fucking free, mate, I'M FREE!'

Adam sat back and tried to weigh up his boss's mental state. Had he flipped?

He asked in a measured, even tone, 'So why were you crying just now, boss? What's with the tears?'

Jack's face fell and he looked suddenly much older, haggard and downcast.

'I'm crying, mate, for all the wasted years. I'm crying for all the girls I could have laid, for all the fun I could have had. I'm crying for all the time I've lost.'

'You selfish bastard. Is that why you were crying? You felt sorry for yourself? What about the rest of us with our fucking wives? What about the rest of us poor sods?'

Jack smiled almost smugly.

'That's up to you, mate. I've done my bit. I've shown the way. And anyway…' He sighed again. 'There's another reason for me to be crying.'

'What's that?' Adam's voice was sullen and resentful.

'I've got the fucking clap. Big red, weeping sores. It's horrible, really painful. But that's what happens when you're having fun.'

⇢ MAY DAY 2004 ⇠

'WE WILL, WE WILL, ROCK YOU!'

The shouting was getting louder as the crowds drew nearer. Sir Oliver strained to look down into the streets below from his tenth floor office. He could see the thin blue lines of riot police stretching across the road, sheltering behind shields and barricades, and supported by armoured water cannons. He was sweating, nervous despite the obviously tight security around the building. A buzzer sounded on his desk.

'Excuse me, Sir Oliver, but Mister Hooker's here to see you.'

'Thank you, June. Send him in.'

Sir Oliver turned to face Dan Hooker, the head of Equity Sales and Trading, an East End boy in the old-fashioned sense of the term.

'Good morning, Dan. Coffee?'

'No. No thanks, Sir Oliver. I just wanted to let you know that the lads are ready, if it comes to it.'

Sir Oliver looked him in the eye.

'Thank you, Dan. I never had any doubt that I could count on your chaps.'

'Are you ready, sir?'

Sir Oliver gestured towards a pair of gleaming Purdy shotguns propped against the sofa.

'I'm ready, Dan. They won't do to me what they did to poor Ben Waring.'

They both nodded and reflected on the fate of Sir Benjamin Waring, head of the family bank of the same name, who had been killed at the previous year's May Day demonstration. The bank's head office had first been stoned, then firebombed and eventually stormed by demonstrators. Sir Benjamin had been chased onto the roof and cornered, and had finally flung himself over the parapet rather than face whatever fate the mob had in mind for him.

'All my lads are here, sir. Even one or two with hangovers. What sort of turnout have we had from the other departments?'

Sir Oliver allowed himself a cynical smile.

'Much as you'd expect. Most of Corporate Finance have stayed away. The clever ones are out of the country on 'business'. The stupid ones are no-shows, ringing in sick or whatever. A hard core of long-serving M and A types showed up, dressed in suits and ties. All Brits, of course.'

'How about Fixed Income? There are a lot of foreigners there.'

'There are, and some have contrived not to be here, but on the whole they've put on a good show. Treasury and Banking are almost all here, and so are Equity Capital Markets. I'd say that overall we're at around eighty percent of normal strength.'

Hooker nodded. 'All right, sir. I'd better get back to the lads. Good luck.'

The two men shook hands and Hooker left to return to the equity trading floor.

Sir Oliver leant over to a bank of newly installed video monitors that showed the outside of the building and – more worryingly – key points inside. He had authorised over two million pounds' worth of additional security expenditure for this year's May Day demonstration. This year, 'Rock Against Capitalism' were specifically targeting Bartons, following the bank's successful raising of a billion – dollar healthcare fund to invest in advances in medical technology and pharmaceutical research. The television news had carried reports of demonstrators filling rucksacks with bricks and stones on which the word 'Bartons' was painted. An initially low-key campaign against the bank had steadily snowballed. Sir Oliver routinely had his mail screened against cranks and terrorists, and travelled in an armoured limousine with two bodyguards. But today was different. Today Bartons were the top target in what had come to be described among anarchist groups as 'the Event'.

'WE WILL, WE WILL, ROCK YOU!!!'

The shouting was louder now, a threatening mass of angry, hate-filled voices. Sir Oliver took up his post at the window once again. He could see the policemen down below stiffen, raise their shields, preparing for what would happen next. And then, around the corner came the crowd. There were thousands of them, filling the street from one side to the other. Many were wearing crash helmets, masks, scarves tied round their faces to hide their identity. Some were carrying placards. They were being marshalled by men with megaphones, who were also orchestrating the chanting. The crowd stopped some twenty yards from the police ranks. The chanting changed.

'What do we want?'

'BARTONS!!'

'What do we want?'

'BARTONS!!'

It was a mind-numbing, dehumanising chant. As Sir Oliver watched, one of the demonstrators stepped forward with a megaphone and walked towards the police lines. He was surrounded by a bevy of cameramen and photographers. Sir Oliver strained to hear as he started to read out a prepared statement.

'We, the people of this country, demand to be heard. We demand that the faceless institutions, the money masters, the wheelers and dealers listen to us! We demand that they stop their war on the environment, on the innocent, on the unprotected. We make these demands in the name of the planet, in the name of the people!'

An opening appeared in the police ranks and an officer in riot gear stepped forward and went to talk to the demonstrator. Around him cameras flashed as the press tried to record what was being said. After a few moments the policeman returned to his own side and the chanting resumed. A buzzer sounded again on Sir Oliver's desk. He walked across and picked up the telephone. It was Nick Hood, Bartons' head of Security, himself an ex-policeman.

'Sir, I've got chief superintendent Richardson with me. He says the demonstrators want to send a delegation to hand in a petition. If we accept, they say they'll walk past peacefully. He thinks they'll still throw stones, but it's better than a pitched battle.'

Sir Oliver paused to think. Could it be a ruse? Undoubtedly. But it was important for the bank to be seen to co-operate fully with the police.

'Very well. Let them send a small delegation with the petition. They can simply hand it in at reception. I have no intention of meeting with these people myself.'

After he had hung up he went to the monitors to observe the scene at reception. The police ranks had parted to allow a small group of demonstrators to approach the main doors to Bartons, where a dozen burly thug-like doormen were waiting – hired for the day by Nick Hood. One of the demonstrators was carrying a large cardboard box, presumably containing the petition, while the others carried placards. As they mounted the steps at the front of the building, one of the placard carriers spoke into a megaphone.

'We come in peace! This is a peaceful demonstration. We are exercising our lawful right to demonstrate! WE COME IN PEACE!!'

What's he saying that for, wondered Sir Oliver. But even as the words were spoken, the meaning of the signal became clear. The demonstrator carrying the cardboard box tipped it up, scattering piles of paper on the steps, and took from underneath a small hand-held machine-gun. There was a 'Drrrrrr' sound as he fired at the security guards, several of whom fell to the ground, while the others scattered. The demonstrator with the gun turned and fired randomly into the police ranks, causing them too to break and scatter. And at the same moment a great roar went up from the crowd – 'WE COME IN PEACE!!' – and they charged forward, hurling a shower of bricks, stones and petrol bombs into the broken police ranks.

Within seconds the scene below had become a confused mass of fighting individuals, the cohesion of the police lost in the face of the machine-gunner. He stood at the top of the steps, grinning and firing randomly, until suddenly he spun around and collapsed. Police marksman, thought Sir Oliver – and a good shot too. But it was too late for Bartons. The surging crowd reached the doors and charged through. The inside monitor showed them vaulting over the security barriers and rushing past the terrified receptionists. Hood and his doormen were overwhelmed. They stood solidly like prop forwards and faced into the crowd, occasionally flooring the invaders with well-aimed punches, but the crowd simply surged past them.

From speakers throughout the building alarm sirens went off and a disembodied voice started saying, 'Attention all staff, attention all staff – demonstrators have entered the building.' Sir Oliver went to the speakerphone by his desk and pressed a button.

'Seal the lifts. Lock all doors and fire exits. Remain at your desks and await police intervention. Do not antagonise the demonstrators, I repeat, no heroics.'

It was too late for that. In the Treasury and Banking Division eight floors below, the mob charged up the stairs and used fire axes to break down the doors into the dealing room. Dealers were dragged from their desks, screens were smashed and fires started. The dealers fought back where they could, but the demonstrators were too many and too well prepared and produced previously concealed weapons

– iron bars, pickaxe handles and knives – which made the dealers' telephone handsets look inadequate by comparison. It was the same story as the demonstrators fought their way to the upper floors. Only in Corporate Finance did they meet their first serious opposition. The department was largely deserted, but as the mob threw open the doors to the UK Mergers and Acquisitions team, they were met with a hail of missiles – bins, chairs, laptops, mobile phones flew through the air, causing several of the demonstrators to fall injured to the ground, while others sought shelter. In his office on the tenth floor Sir Alex watched the monitor with pride as a small group of middle-aged men in pinstriped suits held back the mob. He knew it could only be tempo-rary, and sure enough, there was a shower of flying missiles in the other direction and suddenly flames were billowing up towards the ceiling. One elderly, pinstriped figure ran across the room, his clothes blazing, his mouth open, pre-sumably screaming in agony. There goes poor old Peters, thought Sir Oliver, half guiltily, remembering the previous year's bonus round, when he had personally spoken out against paying the 'old dinosaur' a halfway decent number. He watched as long-haired hippies and shaven-headed thugs in combat clothing swept through the M and A Department, beating and kicking the corporate financiers until they could no longer resist. The mob swept on.

When they reached the Fixed Income and Foreign Exchange floor they again met resistance, though it was patchier and less well organised. Most of the trading desks were organised according to the markets and currencies they served, and typically staffed by nationals of those coun-tries. Thus while some desks were virtually unmanned – the Italian team, for example – others had full turnouts. Sir Oliver watched as the 'Garlic Belt' teams shouted insults at the demonstrators, threw a few missiles and then broke and ran. Soon a crowd of screaming, semi-hysterical Spaniards,

Greeks and Italians were running round the floor, chased by the mob. In the centre of the floor the German team, fully manned, stood firm and silent. Joerg Eisenhart, the managing director in charge of the German business, stood two metres tall, blonde, blue-eyed and broad-shouldered. Military service in the elite Kampfschwimmer, the German army's combat frogmen, had been followed by three years as a professional ice hockey player. As the first screaming, long-haired rioter ran towards him swinging a baseball bat, Eisenhart caught the bat in mid-swing and with one arm slowly pushed it backwards. The rioter stared at him, terrified, and Eisenhart snatched the bat from his grasp, handed it to one of his team, and then picked him up bodily from the floor. He lifted him high into the air, spun around with him and threw him into an oncoming group of demonstrators. At the next desk the sterling bond traders gave a great cheer and waded in beside the Germans, fists flying. For several minutes the scene resembled a classic saloon brawl from an old Western, but then Jean-Claude Dulache and the French team, who had earlier vanished from the floor, charged into the rear of the demonstrators in a vicious ambush, wielding fearsome-looking improvised weapons. The demonstrators broke in the face of the two-sided assault and scattered. The moment of victory was brief, but it was joyful, and for an instant there was a triumphant cheering and mutual backslapping among the teams – something Sir Oliver had never seen before. But then another great shout went up from the staircase – 'WHAT DO WE WANT? BARTONS!!' – and with a great, bestial roar the mob surged forward again. Sir Oliver turned away from the grim scenes.

'Excuse me, Sir Oliver?'

It was June, peering timidly round the door.

'Come in, June. What is it?'

'Mister Hood just called, sir – he says he's got a helicopter to land on the roof to take you and the other board members to safety. It'll be here in five minutes. You need to go up to the roof now, Sir Oliver.'

The look in his eyes was pensive, far away.

'June, I've been nearly forty years at this firm. My father and grandfather were both here before me. I don't think I'm going to let a bunch of wretched eco-terrorists and thugs drive me out now. I'll go down with the ship, if that's what it comes to.' He paused and looked at her thoughtfully. 'June – you've been with me for twenty-three of those years, and you've got a husband and children to think of. You take my place on the helicopter. Here.' He picked up his fountain pen and scribbled a note on his personal headed paper. 'Show this to Mister Hood with my compliments.'

She had tears in her eyes. 'Sir Oliver, I'm so…so worried, so frightened.'

'I know. We're living in strange times.' He put his arms around her and held her, something that for the past twenty-three years would have been unthinkable. 'Go now – quickly, before it's too late.'

She left, weeping, as he turned back to the monitors. All of the lower eight floors had been taken. Many of the windows had been broken and flames were coming from several floors. Outside there was pandemonium, clouds of tear gas were blowing down the street, an ambulance had been overturned and set on fire, fire engines were being stoned as they tried to get through the battling mob. This really is the end, he thought, as the monitor showed him that they had reached the last bastion, the Equities Division.

Down on the ninth floor Dan Hooker had made his final preparations. With the lifts sealed, the only way onto the trading floor was via the stairs at either end. He had taken his best teams – the South African Sales and Trading team and the market-makers who traded the brewing and leisure sector – and put them into the front line to hold the stairs.

Behind them other teams were prepared to deal with any individual demonstrators who fought their way through. Smoke was coming up from the lower floors, and outside the building he could see smoke and flames rising past the windows.

'Here they come! Get ready, lads!'

The words were spoken in a thick South African accent. Hooker turned to the stairs at the north end of the building. A shower of bricks and stones came up from the level below, and one of the South Africans fell to the floor, blood streaming down his face. Then a bottle flew through the air, a burning rag sticking out of its neck.

'Firebomb!'

The warning was too late, as the bottle shattered and flames sprayed around the group of men at the top of the stairs.

'Bastards!' It was Mick van Smit, the head of the South African desk. 'Let's kill 'em!'

'No – stay where you are!' shouted Hooker, but it was too late. The South Africans charged into the mob below – and were swallowed by it. The biggest of them literally dived forward off the top of the stairs to land on top of the crowd below, bringing a dozen of them down. But then the mob surged forward again, trampling friend and foe alike in their bloodlust, and they reached the top of the stairs. The fighting now was at its worst. Those with their wits about them realised that the building was burning beneath them. They were too high for the fire brigade to rescue them, even if fire engines with ladders could get through the crowds. There was nowhere to run, nowhere to hide. And no quarter was asked or given.

From his office on the tenth floor Sir Oliver saw Dan Hooker holding down a screaming, thrashing figure in denim jeans, combat jacket and ski mask. Hooker pulled off the ski mask and brought an industrial-sized stapler down on the youth's contorted face. Hooker was shouting as he leant hard on the stapler once, twice, three times. Each time that Hooker leant forward the youth screamed and writhed more, until after the third time he stopped and lay still, his face covered in blood. Hooker stood to face the mob and another bottle flew through the air, smashing at his feet. He was enveloped in flames and ran across the floor, straight towards the massive plate glass picture windows with their splendid view across the City. He hit the glass with such force that it cracked from top to bottom and shattered, allowing his blazing body to fall nine floors into the crowds below. Poor Dan, thought Sir Oliver, a decent fellow. Now Shenkman from New York will finally get his hands on Equities.

Another screen caught Sir Oliver's eye. It was the rooftop. A large helicopter had landed a few minutes ago, and now the board members were being ushered into it by Hood and some of his thugs. He saw June running out towards the helicopter, holding the piece of paper he had given her. Hood stepped in front of her, shaking his head, and one of his thugs took her by the arm. She was shaking her head, protesting and waving the piece of paper, but then the wind from the helicopter's rotor blades caught it and snatched it from her grasp, to blow away over the side of the building. Hood shook his head forcefully again, and June collapsed, weeping, to the floor. Hood and his thugs boarded the helicopter and it lifted a few feet from the roof just as a group of running figures sprinted into camera shot. One of them threw a petrol bomb that flew through the open door and exploded inside the passenger compartment. The helicopter veered off course, clipped the edge of the building, flipped onto its side and disappeared over the side to explode out of camera shot. Sir Oliver looked on grimly. Good God, he thought, I often said we should wipe the slate clean, but not like this. By the look of those flames we'll need a new building too. Absurdly, the fire sprinklers in his office came on, spraying him with jets of cold water as he sat at his desk, awaiting the final act. He placed his Purdies on the desk in front of him. Both were loaded with solid shot. Outside in the corridor he could hear shouting, the sound of running feet. He stood and raised his shotgun. There was a crash in the outer office, the sound of breaking glass. The magnificent oak double doors to his office flew open and there was a great explosion as he fired...at his wife! It was Lady Sarah. What in God's name was she doing here?

'Sarah? Sarah, darling, is that you?'

'Of course it's me, Oliver! Who do you think it is?'

He looked around, startled. He was lying on the sun lounger beside the pool at Manor Park, his country estate in Hampshire.

'Oliver darling, you fell asleep and you've been dreaming again. Was it that same nightmare? Look at you – you're covered in sweat. I think you'd better go and have a shower. I'll call Rogers to bring us both a cup of tea. Unless you feel you need something stronger?'

He looked at her, baffled. He was soaked.

'What time is it?'

'Oliver, you can see for yourself.' She nodded towards a beautifully engraved sundial next to the pool. 'It's three o'clock in the afternoon.'

Sir Oliver looked at the sundial. It was beautifully ornate, an intricate mixture of brass, copper and gold. There were only two others like it in the world, and he owned both of them – he kept one each next to the pool for London, New York and Tokyo.

'And what day? What date?!'

'Sunday the twenty-seventh of April, 2003,' she said pedantically.

'Phew,' he gasped, breathless. 'At least there's time.'

'Time for what?' she asked him, puzzled.

'Time to hand over to that bastard Collins. He's wanted it for years. Well, now he can have it. One more bonus, cash in my stock options, and then retire.'

She relaxed a little. He sounded more like his old assured self. He turned to her. 'Darling, if you're speaking to Rogers, tell him to bring us a bottle of Krug.' He was staring into the middle distance, his mind contemplating the future. 'Yes. There's a lot to do, but we have time. I definitely think we should be celebrating!'

✦ MERGER ✦

'What we need in Europe is bandwidth!'

Oh God, thought James, *here we go again.* He found the grating American accent almost unbearable. The two men were sitting in James' office overlooking the Broadgate Circle. *A nice office,* thought James, as he stared out at the lunchtime ice-skaters, *it'll be a pity to lose it – and to think of the department moving to Canary Wharf, of all places.*

'And traction! That's the other thing we need. We need bandwidth and traction in Europe. That's why our two boards decided to merge Mordheimer with Bartons.'

What is he talking about – 'bandwidth and traction'? More capacity, perhaps? Greater resources? More stamina? God only knows, and it's not really his fault. He probably doesn't know himself. He's just repeating the latest 'in'-phrase from the current Wall Street guru, the way they all do.

James spoke for the first time.

'I'm interested in your views, Herbert, but I'm not sure that's the way our people see it.'

F. Herbert Bachuber III gave James a long sideways look. He was the taller of the two men by a full head, and was dressed in a classic dark blue Wall Street suit with clashing shirt and tie, red braces and slicked-back hair. James Barker-Smith was altogether more soberly dressed, pinstriped, portly and balding, but comfortable in a faded, lived-in way.

'Well, Jim,' *Jim?! No one calls me Jim,* 'they'd better, that's all I can say, they'd better. If they don't get with the programme, well…' F. Herbert made a cutting gesture across his throat with one forefinger. 'We take no prisoners in this business, you know, Jim, we take no prisoners. That's just not the American way, at least on Wall Street.'

He gave James what was clearly meant to be a meaningful look. *Oh, for God's sake.* James cleared his throat.

'Leaving aside our two countries' respective attitudes towards prisoners of war,' *you pea-brained, one-dimensional oaf,* 'at Bartons we pride ourselves on the way we treat our people. We may not earn as much as you Americans, but our Corporate Finance Department has one of the lowest staff turnover rates in the City. As head of department last year I attended three dinners for members of the department who have served twenty-five years at the firm. We look after our people, and in return they're loyal to us.'

F. Herbert cleared his throat, stood and turned to look out of the window. James could swear he saw the beginnings of a grin on the man's face.

'Well, Jim, all I can say is that the winds of change are going to blow pretty hard through this old City of yours.' He turned and James could see that he was indeed grinning. 'And some of your guys will have a bad case of the wind!' He turned back to the window, chuckling at his joke. 'Jim, people are a commodity. It's been that way on Wall Street for years, and now it's London's turn. You Brits have to get with the programme. We fire the worst-performing ten per cent of our employees routinely every year. But we pay our top performers real money! And that's what we like – incentivisation. We want our people motivated, Jim, so they get out there and generate business. If they don't, they move on. And come to think of it, if they do, they move on too, because they get poached. Stars always get poached. In the past ten years I've worked for six different firms. If someone stayed twenty-five years in the same department at Mordheimers, I'd fire him and his boss, because I'd know that neither of them could be any good.'

James sighed. *Oh dear, this is not going well. Are all department heads going through something like this? What's Sir Oliver thinking about, agreeing to a merger with these people? Talk about no meeting of minds – I don't think these people have minds that we could meet with.*

He leant forward sympathetically. 'But Herbert, if our people simply try to generate transactions for the sake of doing business, our corporate clients will no longer trust us. We have a long tradition of offering impartial advice. We're not salesmen. Our clients know us and respect us and in the long term they reward us well. It's a matter of principle.'

'Bullshit!!!' F. Herbert was suddenly galvanised, striding round the room, almost physically intimidating with his six -foot-odd physique. James stared at him. *What do they feed these people?* 'Jim, let me tell you one thing. On Wall Street it's a matter of principle to have no principles. We live from month to month, quarter to quarter. If your monthly revenue run rate's down on last year, you'd better have a good reason. We live or die by the deals we do. The whole team sweats all year round, every year. No one's comfortable, no one gets complacent.' *Another meaningful look, oh dear. We're clearly not going to get on.*

'Herbert, it's most interesting to hear your views. You obviously run your department here in Europe very differently from the way I run mine.'

'You're damned right, Jimbo!' *Jimbo! Good God, we're definitely not going to get on.* 'And let's not forget that Mordheimer's Corporate Finance revenues are three times those of Bartons.' His words had a crudely threatening tone.

Oh no, let's not play silly numbers games.

'Globally, yes, you're right, Herb.' F. Herbert straightened and raised an eyebrow at the familiar form. 'But the global numbers aren't really a like-for-like comparison, are they?' *Time for my most supercilious, patronising smile – I hope it's not wasted on him.* 'In Europe, our Mergers and Acquisitions practice is three times as big as yours. Obviously, we've never established an American practice, and certainly wouldn't claim to compete with the Wall Street majors such as yourselves.' *Time for a graver, more serious tone.* 'But over here, you've never really cracked it, have you? You're small fry, chasing the scraps from the big boys' tables. Aggressive, yes, and sometimes spectacularly successful, but no consistency. Or am I being unfair?'

How astonishing – he's lost for words. I wonder if he's really American after all. Presumably not used to 'the Limeys' fighting back.

'Just what are you saying, Jim?' F. Herbert almost growled the words. He stepped forward and loomed threateningly over James' desk, staring down at the smaller man. 'Just what the hell are you saying, you pompous, arrogant, small-minded, prissy little Brit?' His jaw was sticking out and he stared venomously at James. James swallowed. *This is getting out of hand. Time to calm things down.*

'Look, Herbert, I don't think we should personalise this, do you? We're going to be colleagues, after all, and it's important that we start off on the right foot.'

'Oh yeah? Well let me tell you, pal – this already is personal! Business is personal. War is personal, and business is like war. Have you read *The Art of War*? Don't tell me, you were too busy studying Shakespeare. Look at the two of us. I work out every day of my life. I train and I sweat, because that's what Americans do. Look at you – you're forty pounds overweight if you're an ounce!'

'Steady on,' interrupted James, 'I play the occasional round of golf, and I do shoot, you know.'

'Steady on,' mimicked F. Herbert, attempting to parody James' indignant response. 'Listen, pal – I'll give you 'steady on'. I'll give you 'steady on' up your arrogant English ass.' He reached inside his jacket pocket and threw a letter down on James' desk. 'These were distributed this morning to the key members of the new senior management team. Read it – you can see who it's from.'

James picked it up. It was on a new joint letterhead – Mordheimer and Barton – and bore the seal of the new joint chief executives, Sir Oliver Barton and Charles Fitzgerald Mordheimer II. James glanced quickly through the text, taking it in and trying desperately not to react. F. Herbert leant forward across the desk so that his face was inches from James'.

'Now let's cut the crap. I've been appointed sole head of Corporate Finance in Europe. I'm the one they've chosen. I'M THE BOSS!' he roared.

James pushed his chair back from the table, creating some distance between the two men.

'So what do you intend to do with the department?' he asked quietly.

F. Herbert laughed and wandered back to the window. He nodded towards one of the ice-skaters. 'Nice ass. You'll miss the view, Jimbo.' He turned back towards James. 'For starters, I'll clean up this mess you've created. Give this place some structure. Have teams organised by industry sector – we'll invest in hiring in top talent from other firms. Get rid of all the smaller clients you've been wasting time on for years – they don't pay enough and they tie up people. Then we're having a big spring-clean.'

He looked meaningfully at James. 'Get rid of the dead wood. Introduce a hurdle rate of fees generated for all directors – anyone who pulls in less than five million bucks a year gets fired!' He sat on the edge of James' desk, gloating, staring down at the smaller man. 'How does it sound so far, Jimbo?'

James leant forward and put his head in his hands.

'Terrible.'

F. Herbert laughed, walked round the desk and slapped James on the back.

'Jimbo, this is only the start.' He was beaming, really getting into his stride. 'One of the key issues is compensation. This whole process has been really unsettling for my people. I'm having to structure some special compensation for my core team – you know the kind of thing, guaranteed bonuses, lock-ins, some kind of stock option golden handcuff arrangement. Just for the key players in the department, of course.'

'What about my people?' asked James.

'Who? Your people? Hey, Jim, let's be real about this. Until I decide whether or not I want them as my people, there's no point locking them in, is there?' F. Herbert laughed, a faraway look in his eyes. 'Jimbo, welcome to the new beginning. All the Brit merchant banks will go this way. They just can't cut it any more. You know, somebody once said that London would be a great city to host the Olympic Games – but don't expect to see any Brits get medals. Well, that's how it is with the City of London.' He laughed and reached inside his jacket to take out a large cigar. *Oh no, not in my office – please!* James pushed his chair back from the desk, got up and walked over to the window. F. Herbert seized the opportunity and sat down in James' chair, pushing it back further so that he could put his feet on the desk while he lit his cigar.

From the window, James stared down at the ice rink.

'You know, I will miss this view, more than I can say.'

F. Herbert shrugged, taking his first puffs on the cigar. 'Life's a bitch, Jimbo. We can't all be winners.'

'You're right.' James reached inside his jacket pocket and pulled out a letter. He tossed it onto the desk. 'Read it – you can see who it's from.'

For the first time F. Herbert looked unsettled. He scanned it once, then twice, and then once more as his jaw dropped open. He stubbed his cigar out in the waste-paper bin.

'Hey…buddy, I had no idea,' he laughed, uncertainly, a look of fear passing across his face, 'but congratulations! This is a big job. And New York, too, I mean, well, hey, this is great news!' He stood, suddenly pale, and walked around the desk, holding his outstretched hand towards James.

James ignored it. He walked over to his desk and retrieved the letter.

'It's ironic, isn't it? It isn't what I wanted at all, but apparently both our chief executives feel that the combined corporate finance franchise needs more of a client focus.' He shrugged. 'I don't think of what I do as having a client focus. I just regard it as common sense. If you look after your clients, they'll look after you.'

'Hey, damned right, buddy – I'm with you!' F. Herbert slapped him on the shoulder.

'It's not sole head, of course,' he paused, looking the other man in the eye. 'It's joint global head, alongside a colleague of yours from Mordheimers, a man called Lewis Jackson. Apparently he hasn't always seen eye to eye with you in the past. They think I might be able to smooth things out a bit.'

F. Herbert was white. James briefly wondered if the other man was about to faint.

'Hey, you know what business is like, old buddy. Lewis and I are just fine – like you and me, really – we're so close, people can't see daylight between us. Joined at the hip!'

James suddenly felt extremely weary.

'Well – perhaps I've been misinformed. More seriously, I will want to discuss your plans in Europe in some detail before I complete my move to the United States.'

'Hey, sure thing, old buddy – and just forget the things I was saying just now. Sometimes I get a bit carried away. It's because I care so much!'

James nodded. 'Thank you, Herbert, that will be all.'

F. Herbert swallowed, looked uncertainly around him, nodded at James and turned to leave. 'Well, congratulations again, old buddy.'

As the door closed James was staring out of the window. *Yes, she does have a nice arse. I'll miss all this.* He walked back to his desk and flicked the intercom.

'Valerie?'

'Yes, Mister Barker-Smith?'

'Valerie, I need to talk to someone from Personnel. I need to know how we fire people in this brave new firm of ours!'

First published in Great Britain by

ELLIOTT & THOMPSON LIMITED
8 Caledonia Street
London N1 9DZ

ISBN 1 904027 04 0

First printed 2002. Reprinted 2002, 2003

Book design by Brad Thompson
Printed and bound by Interprint Limited, Malta